CANTERWOOD
CREST

CHASING BLUE

 JESSICA BURKHART

m!x
ALADDIN MIX
New York London Toronto Sydney

This book is a work of fiction. Any references to historical events, real people, or real locales are used fictitiously. Other names, characters, places, and incidents are the product of the author's imagination, and any resemblance to actual events or locales or persons, living or dead, is entirely coincidental.

ALADDIN MIX

Simon & Schuster Children's Publishing Division

1230 Avenue of the Americas, New York, NY 10020

First Aladdin M!X edition March 2009

Copyright © 2009 by Jessica Burkhart

All rights reserved, including the right of reproduction
in whole or in part in any form.

ALADDIN PAPERBACKS, ALADDIN MIX, and related logo are registered
trademarks of Simon & Schuster, Inc.

For information about special discounts for bulk purchases, please contact Simon
& Schuster Special Sales at 1-866-506-1949 or
business@simonandschuster.com.

The Simon & Schuster Speakers Bureau can bring authors to your live event. For
more information or to book an event contact the Simon & Schuster Speakers
Bureau at 1-866-248-3049 or visit our website at
www.simonspeakers.com.

Designed by Jessica Handelman

The text of this book was set in Venetian 301 BT.

Manufactured in the United States of America

8 10 9

Library of Congress Control Number 2008938581

ISBN 978-1-4169-5841-3

1211 OFF

ACKNOWLEDGMENTS

Alyssa "Fabulous One" Henkin, you've spoiled me by being the smartest, savviest, and sweetest agent on the planet.

Kate "Editor K" Angelella, I bow to your awesomeness! You make every step of this process sparkly and fun.

Jessica "Design Goddess" Sonkin, the cover is beyond fantastic.

Monica "Photographer Extraordinaire" Stevenson, you captured Sasha and friends in the most gorgeous and expressive ways.

Mandy "Music City" Morgan, you rock for responding to my zillion e-mails!

Jason "The Real GamerGuy" Burkhart, you're the reason Jacob's so cool.

Read the first book in the Canterwood Crest series:

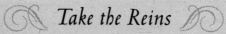 *Take the Reins*

For Jason because you always knew when I needed a break and offered to play Mario Party 6—your least fave game ever—with me because you knew I loved it. Princess Peach!

I

BETTER THAN
LIP GLOSS

"YOU SURE DAD AND I DON'T NEED TO COME with you to your dorm, hon?" Mom asked.

"Nope," I said, grinning at Mom and Dad from the backseat. "I'll be fine."

I looked out the window as my parents' SUV rolled to a stop. It felt as if I were looking at the boarding school's campus for the first time. The gentle Connecticut hills rolled in the distance. A January frost covered the manicured grass and swept sidewalks. The stable roof peeked over the hill.

Nothing could have made me more excited than my first day back at Canterwood Crest Academy after Christmas break. Not even if I'd won a year's supply of free lip gloss—and that's saying something. I couldn't wait to see Charm—I planned on going to see him as soon as I dropped my bag at my dorm.

Dad turned to look at me, but his stomach, rounded from too many spicy chicken wings, caught on the steering wheel.

"Okay," he said. "Let's get your bag."

I felt a chill as soon as my boot hit the frozen pavement, but it wasn't from the cold. I'd missed Canterwood—especially Charm and my friends—so much.

Dad popped the trunk open and reached inside for my oversize L.L. Bean duffel bag.

"Won't you need help unpacking?" Mom asked. She put her hands on the hips of her non–Mom jeans (the ones I'd convinced her to buy over break) and stared at me.

"I'm already moved in," I said. "All I have to unpack are my clothes and my laptop."

This was *nothing* like September, when I'd first come to Canterwood for seventh grade. I'd needed my parents every step of the way, from unpacking to attending orientation. Now, I felt like a pro. Maybe a new student would even ask me for directions.

"We'll miss you, sweetie," Dad said, hugging me tightly. "I'm sure Mom will call you in . . ." He looked at his watch. ". . . fifteen to twenty minutes."

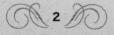

I laughed and hoisted my heavy bag over my shoulder. After a few more assurances that we would see each other soon, that I wouldn't forget to eat, and that I'd call if I needed anything, Mom and Dad got in the SUV and drove out of the parking lot, disappearing down the Canterwood driveway.

I shifted my bag and set off for my dorm in Winchester A. Butkis Hall, which everyone just called Winchester for obvious reasons. Inside the dorm, chatter filled the hallway and girls ran up to each other, giggling and hugging after the long winter break away from each other. When I'd moved into Winchester last fall, I'd hated the bright yellow hallway walls. Now, I touched the wall and smiled. It was good to be home.

I peered inside Livvie's office, but it was empty. Livvie, our dorm monitor, was probably helping someone move in or assuring a parent that she had plenty of rules (#67 in the handbook) to keep us out of trouble.

I dodged a pile of red suitcases and stopped outside the door with the familiar bubbly pink sign reading SASHA AND PAIGE. I opened the door and peeked inside.

"Paige!"

"Sasha!" Paige squealed. "Hi!" Paige Parker, my friend and roommate from Manhattan, looked stylish as usual

in indigo skinny jeans and a soft camel-brown cashmere sweater. She dropped her textbooks on her desk and ran over to hug me.

I let my bag fall to the ground.

"You totally disappeared over break!" I said. We'd texted and chatted on the phone until a few days ago. Then I'd gotten a cryptic text from Paige that had said, *Gonna be MIA till school. Mom's stressing family time. Save me!!*

Paige groaned. "I know! Sorry. I thought Mom was *finally* going to let me watch TV for once. But all I got to see was *The History of Christmas* on PBS. In. Two. Four. Hour. Segments."

"Yikes. Well, that sounds . . . interesting?"

"Oh, especially the hour-long talk on the origin of the evergreens from Washington's largest tree farm." Paige sat on the end of my bed and watched as I hauled my bag in front of my closet and started unpacking. She stuck out her bottom lip and widened her green eyes.

"Oh, I know what you want," I said with an evil grin. "You want all of my *Southampton Socialite* episodes."

"Please, pretty please!" She fell to her knees as if she were at Mass. Hmmm . . . maybe I could get a batch of her homemade chocolate chip cookies out of this. . . .

"I don't know . . . ," I said in a singsong voice.

"Sasha!" Paige wailed. "I need brain-rotting TV! Now!"

I laughed, rifling through my bag for the DVDs. "They're all yours. But I've got to get to the stable. Callie and I made plans to race!"

The word "race" made my heart pound. My gelding, Charm, was a Thoroughbred/Belgian mix. He loved to run—especially against other horses. It was the perfect way to start the rest of the school year.

I held the DVDs out to Paige. She took them and kissed the covers. "Thank you, thank you! Oh, and I already told Suichin and Annabella that we're watching a movie tonight after our welcome-back meeting with Livvie. Invite Callie, too, if you want."

"Cool." A movie night sounded great. And I'd missed my floormates, Annabella and Suichin—it would be great to see them again.

I plucked my buzzing phone from my pocket and flipped it open.

Hey, Sash! R U on campus yet? Want 2 meet up 4 ice cream ltr? —Jacob

"Jacob wants to meet me," I said.

Paige looked up from the DVD cover she was reading. "He *like*-likes you," she sang.

I rolled my eyes at Paige as I texted him back.

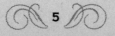

5

Got 2 take care of Charm first, but I'll text U when I'm done.

Unpacking could wait until tonight. If I hurried, I could squeeze in a ride with Callie *and* see Jacob before Livvie's first Winchester meeting of the semester. The meeting would be the usual—basically, a list of rules. No boys in dorms, bed by ten thirty, study every free second of the day. Last semester, Livvie had even told us that reading while we brushed our teeth was a great way to get in an extra two minutes of studying in the morning.

I grabbed a pair of breeches from my drawer and slid into them. Mom and Dad had gotten me new paddock boots for Christmas and the dark brown leather gleamed against my fawn-colored breeches.

"See you at the meeting," I said to Paige.

"'Kay," Paige said, tearing her eyes away from the TV for about three seconds and then turning back. "Win for Winchester!"

"I will!"

I hurried out the door and headed down the Winchester hallway.

On the corkboard near the exit, a pink heart-shaped flyer with fancy lettering caught my eye.

CALLING ALL 7TH & 8TH GRADERS

*Sweetheart Soirée — the only place to be
on Valentine's Day.*

I checked the back of the flyer for more information, but that was it. No time, place, or even website to check for details. I made a mental note to ask Paige about that when I got back.

Outside, in the freezing cold, students and their parents still packed the campus. The newbies hugged their parents and struggled not to cry. The returning students smiled, waved good-bye, and ran off to reunite with their Canterwood friends. Last September I had been a wreck on move-in day, and it had started with a disaster. But today was different.

I wasn't Union Sasha anymore. Canterwood Sasha was here to chase blue championship ribbons, make good grades, and hang out with her new best friends. I dug into my pocket, pulled out my favorite Bonne Bell lip gloss— Dr Pepper—and smoothed some on.

Another thing Canterwood Sasha was here to do? Win the race!

2

US VS. THEM

"CALLIE!" I SQUEALED, THEN QUICKLY GLANCED over my shoulder. If Mr. Conner heard me screaming in the stable, I'd be in trouble for sure.

"Sasha!" Callie left Black Jack, her Morab gelding, crosstied in the aisle and ran up to me. We hugged and I walked over to pat Black Jack's shoulder.

"It's sooo good to be back!" I twirled in a circle and breathed in the horsey scent. "Everything is the same," I said cheerfully. I wanted to see every inch of the place again from the tack room to the hot walker. The sweet scent of clean hay wafted through the air and the stable was warm against the winter chill.

"Did you think the stable changed in the three weeks we were away?" Callie asked.

"It might have," I said. "Look, the nameplates are brighter."

Callie peered at the gold nameplate on one of the lesson horses' stall door. "You're a weird girl, Sasha Silver."

"But that's why you love me," I agreed. "We'll be ready in ten."

"Deal," Callie said.

I ran to Charm's stall and swiped a cotton lead line off the hook on the wall.

"Charm?" I called into the roomy box stall. He lifted his chestnut head from his hay net. Stalks of hay stuck out from the corners of his mouth. "Silly boy," I said, unlatching the stall door. Charm stepped over to me and head-butted my arm. He whickered softly and let me stroke his cheek. He sniffed my hair.

"I missed you, too," I whispered, wrapping him up in a hug. "Let's get you out of here and go for a ride."

Charm bobbed his head in agreement.

I led him out of the stall and examined every inch of him. "Wow," I said. "Mike and Doug took excellent care of you." Charm's chestnut coat gleamed like a new penny. His blaze was blinding white and his hooves were clean. I'd have to remember to thank Mike and Doug, the stable's grooms, for taking such good care of him while I was away.

"One more hug," I said. Charm leaned his neck into me. "Okay, time to tack up!"

A few minutes later, Charm and Jack were tacked up and ready. Outside, Callie and I halted the horses, put on our helmets, and prepared to mount.

I slipped my left foot into the stirrup and was about to push myself up from the ground when I heard hoofbeats behind me.

Heather Fox, Julia Myer, and Alison Robb—aka the Trio—gazed down at me from atop their horses. All of the girls wore fawn breeches tucked into shiny black boots.

"Ready yet?" Heather asked me, her blue eyes narrowed. Her perfect blond hair hung in two loose braids.

"For what?" I asked. I lifted myself into Charm's saddle and turned him to face the Trio. Callie mounted and edged Black Jack beside Charm.

Julia rolled her eyes. "For the race." Her bay mare, Trix, pawed the ground and snorted.

"Callie invited us," Heather said, her lips curling into a barely there smirk.

I twisted in the saddle, turning to Callie. "You did?" I whispered.

Callie shrugged. "They were riding anyway, so I thought it would be fun to race them."

"Okay," I said to the Trio. "Let's go," I squeezed my knees against Charm's sides and urged him forward. Now Charm and I *really* had to win.

"How about we line up behind that fence post?" Alison suggested. She pointed to the edge of the fence line.

The five of us nodded at each other and eased our horses into a line.

I crouched forward and stared between the chestnut tips of Charm's ears. The five horses shifted and tensed as we steadied them in the back pasture. Icy wind whipped my hair back and I shivered beneath my plaid coat.

"We're racing on three and we go until we hit the woods," Heather said from her spot on my right. Her copper-colored Thoroughbred gelding, Aristocrat, flexed his neck and strained against the reins. Charm eyed him before staring ahead. He knew as well as I did that we had to beat them. There was no way I could come back after winter break and lose to Heather.

"One," called Callie. She shifted over Jack's saddle.

"Two," said Julia. She lowered herself over Trix's neck.

"Three!" shouted Alison.

We heeled our horses forward. Alison's palomino, Sunstruck, dashed ahead for an early lead.

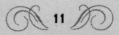

Charm surged forward with such force, he almost threw me back in the saddle. I grabbed a hunk of mane and steadied myself. His muscles had grown since we'd started training at Canterwood last September. His gallop hadn't been half as fast back then.

"Go, go!" I shouted. My hands inched up along his neck and I leaned forward in a jockey's crouch. The brisk wind stung my eyes, but I asked Charm for more speed. Horses rushed around us in a cloud of black, bay, palomino, and chestnut.

Aristocrat's hooves pounded beside me. The gelding edged his nose in front of Charm's. Charm rolled an eye to look at his rival and dug his hooves into the ground, fighting to keep his nose in front. Dark fence rails flashed by us. The horses galloped past the boys' dorms at the south end of campus. Quickly, I ducked my head under my arm and looked back. A couple of yards behind me, Alison and Julia battled for fourth place. Callie and Black Jack pulled even with Aristocrat's flank.

Heather and I were fighting for first—of course. Our eyes connected before Heather dropped herself lower over Aristocrat's neck and yelled, "Go!" He turned on another burst of speed and challenged Charm to catch him. The horses galloped full out. We perched precariously over

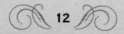

their necks. One misstep and we'd be pitched to the ground. But it was too late to think about that now. Charm wouldn't fall. *Run, Charm!* I thought. *We can't lose!*

Charm stretched his legs into a flying gallop and the wind in my ears drowned out the sound of the other horses. Charm's long strides churned up the frozen grass. I let him out one more notch, but that was it. I didn't want him to get hurt. The woods, rushing toward us, were a few yards away. Chunks of mud flew from Charm's hooves. Mud clods had to be pelting Julia and Alison.

"C'mon, boy!" I urged Charm. He found another gear and pushed to stick his head in front of Aristocrat. Charm and I were going to pull off a win! The tree line loomed closer and Aristocrat fought to catch Charm.

Suddenly, a black blur zoomed past Aristocrat and jumped ahead of Charm. Callie and Black Jack surged past us on the outside and galloped through the clearing. I'd thought they were way behind us! A spray of mud flew through the air and specks landed on my face and thwacked against my helmet. Charm shuddered for a second and hesitated when mud hit his face. He shook it off and lurched forward, chasing Jack. Callie's red coat with a white heart on the back looked like a target racing ahead of us. We were almost there! Aristocrat

swung wide around a tree and lost ground. He ran back by Charm's flank.

"Go, boy!" We could still catch them! Charm's gallop lengthened and he pulled his head even with Jack's. Callie and I turned our heads to look at each other. Neither one of us was giving up. She looked away and urged Jack with her hands. Jack got his nose in front of Charm's. Charm fought to keep up.

I clicked to Charm. We tried to catch Callie and Jack, but the invisible finish line between two boulders at the wood's edge was too close. Jack thundered over the grass between the rocks and Callie pulled him to a canter as they headed into the woods. Aristocrat and Heather crossed a second after Charm and me.

Callie won.

How had that even happened? She'd been behind three seconds ago!

Charm yanked against the reins, frustrated over our loss. "It's okay, boy," I whispered to him. Julia and Alison galloped in behind us. We slowed the horses to a quick trot and let them cool down. When the dirt trail began to narrow, we pulled them to a walk. The horses, exhilarated by the run, tossed their heads and stretched their legs. Charm shook his head and huffed.

"That was so fun!" Julia said. She pulled a compact out of her pocket and checked her reflection. She flicked a speck of dirt off her cheek and passed the mirror to Alison, who held it out to admire the tiny diamond studs in her ears.

"Wow, where did you come from?" I asked Callie. "I thought Jack was running flat out and then you shot by us."

Callie rubbed Jack's neck. "I rated him until the final strides and then let him out all the way."

"Nice one." I tried to hide my frown. I didn't know she was using actual jockey strategy in our race. Heather soothed Aristocrat, who tossed his head and crabstepped. He wanted to run more.

"You totally kicked our butts, Callie," Heather said.

Hmm. She was being awfully gracious about losing. Suspicious.

While everyone started chatting about school, I let Charm ease back a few strides. I'd been so focused on beating Heather, Callie had slipped right by us. Charm and I had underestimated her. But I couldn't be mad at her for winning. Callie and Jack were a great pair and they'd beaten us. So why did it bug me so much? Callie dropped back to ride with me while the Trio ambled a few strides ahead of us.

We reached the top of a hill and looked down at Canterwood's campus. From here, I could see the tennis courts, the closed outdoor swimming pool, the lacrosse field and the stable. Our outdoor dirt ring, cross-country course and dressage arena had a few older riders practicing. My disappointment over losing lifted as I took in the campus.

"It looks *so* much less intimidating from here," Alison said. She stroked Sunstruck's mane and rode closer to Julia. "But when we get back down there . . ." She was right. Canterwood Crest Academy, known for its fierce academic reputation and even tougher athletics, looked small and quiet from atop the hill. But once classes started back up, it would be back to cut-throat competition, studying day and night.

"No kidding," Heather murmured. She pushed back her helmet and revealed her golden, sun-kissed face. It looked like she had spent her winter break on a tropical beach somewhere.

The Trio urged their horses ahead of me and Callie. I thought about how it had been among the five of us at the beginning of the year, my first few months here at Canterwood. Callie and I had become instant BFFs, but it had seemed like the Trio was out to get me from the very beginning—Heather had even put signs up instructing me toward the wrong meeting place for our very first team meeting.

But once we found out we'd all made the advanced riding team, things had calmed down. It was like now that we were an actual team, we had to start acting like it—for the good of our riding. And now it even seemed . . . more or less peaceful.

"What did everyone do over break?" I called out, deciding to take advantage of everyone's good mood.

Julia and Alison didn't hesitate.

"My parents took me to Bermuda," Julia bragged. "We snorkeled and rode horses on the beach."

Alison slowed Sunstruck in front of me. "I hung out at my sister's apartment in NYC and went to her New Year's Eve party. She let me stay up late." Alison turned around in her saddle for emphasis. "Till two."

Behind the Trio, Callie and I rolled our eyes. "What about you?" I asked Heather. "Did you go to Bermuda and stay up till two?"

She looked over her shoulder and glared. "Sasha, we're only trail riding to give the horses a break from campus. Don't start acting like we're BFFs."

I held my heart with mock surprise. "We aren't?"

Callie snickered.

Okay, maybe "peaceful" wasn't the word.

"Well, if you're so obsessed with me and just have to know what I did over break, I'll tell you," Heather said. "My parents bought me a stack of presents, and then ditched me for Christmas morning. Satisfied?"

"Oh," I said. "Sorry."

Mr. Fox, with a heart two sizes smaller than the Grinch's, wasn't exactly Dad of the Year. If he wasn't bossing Heather around about grades or riding, he was totally focused on his business. The man had at least three cell phones and probably talked on all of them at once.

"Movie tonight at Winchester," I whispered to Callie. "Want to come?"

Callie nodded and her black ponytail bounced. "Sounds good—I'll bring the junk food," she said.

I checked my watch as I posted to Charm's trot. Charm's legs and chest were flecked with mud—it would take forever to brush it out. I'd never make it to meet Jacob now. I'd text him later.

Even though we'd texted a few times over break, the last time I'd seen Jacob was at the winter dance, when we'd danced together pretty much all night. I'd had such an amazing time—especially since I'd been crushing on him

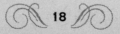

all semester . . . but then we'd both had to go back home for break. Now, I wasn't sure what to expect. Was he my boyfriend? My friend? And even though we didn't have time to meet up today, I figured that maybe not seeing me for another day would make Jacob miss me more and he'd be even more excited to see me in class.

Charm trotted ahead and I followed the sound of jangling to the silver heart charm bracelet glinting off Alison's wrist. I flashed back to the poster I'd seen in Winchester.

"Hey, do you know what the Sweetheart Soirée is?" I asked Callie.

"Supposedly," she said. "It's some big Valentine's Day party for seventh and eighth graders. Very secretive. No one in Orchard Hall knows much. But I bet Heather knows something about it. If anyone does, she will."

I angled Charm beside Heather. She glared at me and Aristocrat laid back his ears when he saw Charm. I knew I'd probably—no *definitely*—regret asking her but, I was too curious to let it go.

"Do you know anything about the Sweetheart Soirée?" I asked Heather. I braced myself for a rude response.

Julia and Alison looked amused.

"You wish, Silver," Heather said. "It's for people who actually have a chance at a date for Valentine's Day." She

let out the reins and Aristocrat propelled into a smooth canter with Trix and Sunstruck flanking him. I rolled my eyes, but Callie and I didn't waste a second before charging after them.

When I got Charm warm, dry, and into his stall, I pulled out my cell and texted Jacob.

Sorry, I can't make it. Took 2 long 2 clean Charm. C U soon?

My phone dinged a few seconds later.

No prob. Ttyl!

My new goal: uncover the secrets behind the Sweetheart Soirée, and see if a certain someone has a valentine . . .

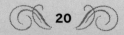

3

THE NEW GUY

PAIGE WAS OFFICIALLY OBSESSED.

It was superearly on frigid Sunday morning and while I dressed for my riding team meeting, she was fixated on writing an essay. On. A. Sunday.

"You sure you don't want to wait until tomorrow to do that?" I asked. "We still have twenty-four hours before school officially starts again. Then we'll *have* to do homework on the weekends."

"This is a BIG deal, Sash!" Paige said. "It's The Food Network for Kids! The essay has to be perfect or they won't even watch my demo DVD."

Paige had decided to try out again to be the new host of *Teen Cuisine*. It was the hottest show on The Food Network for Kids.

"If you want," I offered, "I can help you with the DVD. The judges will love it."

Paige played with the blue chopsticks that held her golden-strawberry hair in a loose bun. "You think?"

"Absolutely." I rifled through my desk and found my favorite pen with pink ink. "Here. Write with this—it'll bring you luck!"

Paige took the pen. "Thanks. See you after your meeting?"

I nodded and left Paige scribbling on her paper. It was stable time.

Heather, Julia, and Alison were already seated and waiting in the small office off the indoor riding arena. They were *always* here first for meetings.

Callie sat beside me.

"Welcome to the seventh grade advanced riding team's first unmounted meeting," our coach, Mr. Conner said. He stepped inside and closed the door. "This semester, we'll have a few unmounted meetings when necessary. I'll call these meetings when we have pressing topics to discuss—such as training techniques or other related matters."

The five of us nodded.

Mr. Conner sat on an uncomfortable-looking wooden chair and peered at the clipboard in his lap.

"The first thing we need to discuss is the show," he said. "It will take all of our time and energy to prepare for this show in the next several weeks." Callie and I eyed each other. Charm loved shows—especially the crowd. Cheering energized him and he loved to show off. "On the first weekend of February, the six of us will be going to Fairfield to compete in the Junior Equestrian Regionals. I received the good news yesterday."

"What?" Callie yelped. "No way!"

Regionals were *huge*. I had only ever dreamed about watching the competition in person—much less riding!

"This show is the biggest event of the year for young riders in New England," Mr. Conner continued. "There will be scouts for the Youth Equestrian National Team and admissions officers for leading workshops and clinics. Riders who do well here could qualify for nationals in the fall."

W.O.W. *Nationals!*

"We have a month to train, so from this point forward, I expect all of you to step it up."

We all nodded. Even the Trio looked excited.

"On weekdays," he said, "you'll be riding before and

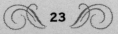

after class. On weekends, your schedule is up to you—unless I call a special meeting."

Julia raised her hand.

"Yes, Julia?" Mr. Conner said.

"How many classes will we show in?" she asked, twirling a lock of her platinum blond bob around her finger.

"Two," he said. "We're training in all three areas—show jumping, dressage and cross-country—but for this show, two classes each will be plenty. In group lessons, we'll work all three areas and in pairs sessions, we'll focus on your specialties."

Pairs sessions?

Callie leaned into me. "What're you showing in?"

"I'll probably do show jumping and cross-country," I whispered. "What about you?"

"Dressage and maybe hunter under saddle. I need a break from cross-country."

Mr. Conner gave his clipboard to Alison. "You should each know your strengths by now. Go ahead and jot them down next to your name."

Alison flipped her long, dark hair over her shoulder and scribbled something down. She passed the clipboard to Heather who wrote down her preferences and passed it along. Julia did the same and then handed me

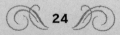

the clipboard. I scanned the list. Heather had written down cross-country and dressage, Alison had signed up for hunter hack and dressage and Julia had marked down hunter hack and show jumping.

Next to my name, I wrote *show jumping and cross-country*. Callie took the clipboard and wrote down dressage and hunter under saddle. She gave the clipboard to Mr. Conner. He read over our choices.

"I've taught you well," he said with a grin. "Now, I want to break you up into pairs and when I cannot conduct lessons, you'll work with your partner. You'll be paired according to your strengths and weaknesses." Mr. Conner consulted his clipboard.

"Julia, you're one of our best jumpers, so you'll be working with Alison who is a strong dressage rider," Mr. Conner said. Julia and Alison high-fived.

Callie and I looked at each other. Mr. Conner wouldn't break us up, would he?

"Sasha, you've got a strong jumping seat," Mr. Conner started. "You'll be working with Heather, who is an exceptional dressage rider."

What? No!

When Mr. Conner looked away, I looked over at Heather. She stared straight ahead, not blinking. Impossible to read.

Mr. Conner smiled at Callie. "I've left Callie without a partner. Since she's equally strong in dressage and jumping, Callie is going to alternate between the two groups."

Heather's glossy mouth fell open. Mine almost did the same. Callie was a fantastic rider, but was she really better than Heather? The look on Heather's face suggested she didn't think so. It would be weird to take directions from Callie *and* Heather.

I nudged Callie. "You have to keep Heather from trotting me to death," I whispered.

Callie hooked her pinky to mine. I tried to shake off my insecurity and be happy for her. Callie was one of my best friends and she always worked hard. She deserved recognition from Mr. Conner.

Mr. Conner smiled at us and put his clipboard on the table. "Please remember, you need to have at least a B average to go to regionals. I need every single one of you to be sure and keep up your grades. Okay?"

We all nodded.

"All right, see you at your next lesson," Mr. Conner said.

We got up and headed for the door.

I took Charm out of his stall and clipped him to the

crossties. His coat still wasn't shiny enough after the mud slinging yesterday that had kept me from meeting Jacob. We'd wanted to meet today instead, but we were both busy. I was actually kind of glad—I needed the extra day to wash my hair again and choose the perfect outfit. Tonight, Paige and I were making egg and banana facials—Paige promised pore tightening and complexion brightening. I'd settle for not getting a giant zit before seeing Jacob for the first time this semester!

As I groomed Charm, my mind drifted back to what Mr. Conner had said about grades. I didn't even want to *think* about my fall report card. Before Canterwood, I had been a straight-A girl, but my first Canterwood report card included half of the alphabet! As, Bs, and an ugly, glaring C+ in biology.

I'd been embarrassed to show it to Mom and Dad. I'd never gotten a C before—ever. But they had said they'd understood. I was at a new school and they expected me to take a semester to settle into classes and life at boarding school. But I'd vowed never to get another C. EVER. AGAIN.

Charm snorted and tugged on the crossties. I looked up and saw that a guy about my age was walking toward us. He stopped in front of Charm.

"Hey," he said, flashing a smile that popped against his deep brown skin. His jet-black hair was tousled. I wondered what he was doing here—he didn't look like a rider in his graphic tee and worn, vintage jeans. Then I spotted his paddock boots.

"Hey—I'm Eric," he said. "Seventh-grade transfer student. As if that wasn't obvious."

I laughed. "Don't worry—it's not obvious. I'm Sasha," I said. "I'm a seventh grader, too." Eric walked up to Charm and offered him a hand to smell. "He yours?" Eric asked.

I nodded. "That's Charm."

Eric's eyes ran over Charm's legs, barrel, and chest. "He has great conformation," Eric said. "You can really see his Thoroughbred lines."

I smiled. Charm loved the word "Thoroughbred"—Eric would forever be his BFF. Charm stretched his neck to Eric and got his pink and black muzzle rubbed.

"Did you bring your own horse?" I asked.

Eric shook his head and I saw a sparkle in his dark brown eyes. "I'm riding school horses for now, but I want my own horse soon."

"Nothing beats having your own horse. Are you finding your way around the stable?" I remembered my first few days here and how easy it had been to get lost on Canterwood's sprawling campus.

Eric smiled. "I think I'm okay. But if you see me looking lost during classes tomorrow . . ."

"I'll point you in the right direction," I finished.

"Thanks," Eric said. He gave Charm a final pat and disappeared down the aisle.

I let myself into my dorm and found stacks of dozens— no, maybe *hundreds*—of recipe and dessert books open and strewn around the dorm. They covered both beds, and almost every inch of the floor.

"Paige?" I called. I tried not to knock over any of the stacks. "Did a book swallow you?"

"No," a voice muttered from behind a pile of books in the corner. "I just can't find *the* recipe."

"I'll help after I shower," I said. I pulled off my boots and hopped over a book pile to get to the bathroom door.

Paige peeked at me from *Just Desserts*. "It has to be perfect," she said, sounding a bit panicked.

"It will be," I soothed. "We'll stay up all night until we find the right recipe."

"We have to go to bed at ten thirty," Paige reminded me.

"Okay, we'll stay up till ten thirty!"

"What if we pick a top four and I'll let you taste them?"

"If I *have* to taste, let's do top ten," I said.

"Deal!" Paige said.

We both burst into giggles. I was glad to be back at Canterwood with Charm and all my friends.

SCORE WAR

THE GLEAM IN MR. CONNER'S EYES SUGGESTED today's practice would be tough.

"Good morning!" Mr. Conner's voice boomed in the indoor arena as we finished our warm up. When the arena was heated, it smelled like horsehair and hay—bad for Alison's allergies. She sneezed nonstop and caused Sunstruck to shake his head in annoyance.

"Everyone ready to get started?" Mr. Conner asked.

Callie, Alison, Julia, Heather, and I nodded from our horses' backs. It was almost seven on a frigid Monday morning and we had forty minutes of practice before we went back to our dorms to change and run to class.

Mr. Conner walked around the arena and pointed to

four stadium jumps. "This morning, we're going to work on show jumping."

He stuck his hands in his black parka. "But this practice is going to be a little different than most."

The Trio, Callie, and I eyed each other for a second.

"Instead of me giving you feedback, *you're* going to score each other," Mr. Conner said. "On a scale from one to ten, you'll score how you think each rider completed the course. Watch for speed, hesitation, form, and approach."

I had to stop myself from groaning out loud—Heather was going to give me a zero. Or a negative two.

Callie and I frowned at each other. The Trio was going to knock us no matter what.

Mr. Conner strode over to us. "You'll need to explain your score after you give it—a one-sentence answer about your choice will do. Callie, you're up first."

"Good luck," I whispered.

"Start on my go," Mr. Conner instructed Callie.

She pushed down her white practice helmet and straightened Black Jack in front of the first vertical with blue and white poles. Mr. Conner pressed the red buzzer in his hand and Callie and Jack cantered forward. Callie sat still and allowed Jack to eye the first jump and then soar over it. She gathered Jack in collected canter and pointed him over a faux brush jump. Jack leapt the plastic greenery with inches to spare and yanked his head once—tugging the reins through Callie's fingers. Callie sat deep in the saddle and tightened the reins before allowing Jack to take off over the liverpool and hop over the final vertical.

Mr. Conner always deducted us for rushing or losing focus, but Callie hadn't done any of that. She slowed Jack to a trot and lined up with us. The four simple fences hadn't winded Jack a bit and he struck the ground with his front hoof—eager to take the course again.

"Scores, please," Mr. Conner said. He pointed to me.

"Eight," I said. "Jack drifted for a second, but you easily got him under control."

"Seven," Julia said. She shifted Trix's reins from one hand to the other. "Jack rushed the third jump and he almost tugged the reins out of your hands once."

Callie frowned slightly, but didn't say a word.

"Seven, too," Alison offered. She pulled at the end of her ponytail. "You could have circled him before taking the last fence. I think he needed extra time."

All of our gazes went to Heather.

"Three."

Oh, *please.* I folded my arms across my chest and glared

33

at Heather. A bucketful of cold water to dump on her head would be nice.

"Three?" Callie sputtered.

"You're lucky," Heather interrupted. "I was going to say two, but I didn't want to completely crush you."

"But—" Callie started.

"Callie," Mr. Conner cut in. "Don't defend. Just listen. You can talk when Heather's finished."

Heather glared at Callie with arched eyebrows. "Black Jack wasn't collected, he didn't pay attention to your cues, and you had to work *way* too hard just to get him over four simple fences. Obviously, you didn't practice once over break."

Ouch. But now that I'd heard her explanation, I realized Heather was right. Callie hadn't been in control.

Callie's face reddened. She urged Black Jack forward until he stood next to Aristocrat. "I practiced every day over break at my old stable," Callie argued. "Jack may have acted up, but our ride wasn't even close to a three. You're just jealous."

"Girls," Mr. Conner called. He waved the clipboard in the air. "That's enough. This is not the point of the exercise. No arguing with your judges. Listen to your scores, but don't defend your ride. Use this as a critique circle. Julia, please get ready."

Julia and Trix breezed through the course. We all gave Julia eights and she whispered, "Yes!" when we were finished. Trix's bay coat didn't even have a hint of sweat.

Alison rode next. Sunstruck took the course easily, but Alison couldn't keep the hot-blooded Arabian's head down. Everyone, even Heather, gave her a seven and she nodded in agreement.

"Heather," Mr. Conner said. He watched from the side of the arena. "You're up."

Smiling under her helmet, Heather pulled on Aristocrat's reins until he lowered his head and backed up straight to the starting line. I couldn't even get Charm to back like that yet.

Heather's slim legs gripped the new Christmas present I'd heard her talking to Julia and Alison about before practice—a gorgeous, supple Stübben eventing saddle. She settled herself into the expensive leather. Mr. Conner hit the buzzer and Aristocrat shot forward. Heather wasn't even pushing him. His taut muscles rippled beneath his shiny coat and, unbelievably, he looked even better than he had last month. He was focused and agile, and he took the jumps as if they were ground poles. Heather guided him over the second, third, and final jump. Aristocrat's ears flicked back, awaiting any

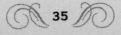

command from Heather, and he didn't lose focus for a millisecond. Per-fect.

With a triumphant smile, Heather pulled Aristocrat to a stop in front of us and he tossed his mane and eyeballed Charm. Charm raised his head and mouthed the bit. He knew we had to beat them.

"Julia," Mr. Conner said. "Your score."

"Ten," Julia said confidently. "You guys were amazing."

Alison nodded. "Ten. He listened to every command and your signals were invisible."

With a small sigh, Callie whispered, "Ten. Good job." If Heather had just knocked me like she had Callie, I don't know if I could have given her a ten.

"Ten," I muttered. "He was fast, but didn't rush. And you went with him instead of over-controlling him."

"I agree," Mr. Conner chimed in, causing Heather's grin to widen. "Excellent ride. Okay, Sasha. Your turn."

"Ready, boy?" I whispered to Charm. He dipped his head and stepped up to the starting line. After losing to Callie during our race, we had to do this right. But four jumps were harder than ten. With four, we couldn't miss one or we'd look bad. Mr. Conner had specifically designed the short course to make us work harder.

Staring forward, I gripped Charm's reins and shoved

my heels down in the stirrup irons. *Four jumps*, I whispered to myself. Just four.

The buzzer sounded. I tapped my boots against Charm's sides. He surged forward and we cantered to the first jump. I lifted out of the saddle and signaled Charm to jump. He bounded over the blue and white poles. He slowed, gathered himself and eyed the second one. His hooves pounded the arena dirt and he tucked his front legs and lifted over the brush jump. The water jump was next. I tightened my legs around Charm's barrel, clicked and urged him forward. "You've got this, boy, c'mon," I whispered. I counted down the strides—*three, two, one*. On one, Charm pushed off from his back hooves and propelled over the liverpool. He didn't even blink at the blue plastic "water" below.

All right! "Yes," I whispered, stroking his neck quickly with one hand. "Good boy!" Charm hopped over the last fence and tossed his head. We trotted back to Callie and the Trio.

"Awesome!" Callie called.

Charm pranced past Aristocrat and we halted next to Black Jack.

"Callie, you first," Mr. Conner said. He put his clipboard on the table.

"Nine," Callie said, "Sasha let Charm have his head, but she was still in control every second."

Julia gave me a small smile. "Nine. Charm was ready for every jump."

Alison opened her mouth and then looked at Heather. Heather glared at her. "Eight," Alison whispered. "You, um, you hesitated before the water jump."

I knew that wasn't true, but there was no point in arguing.

Heather undid her chinstrap. "Six," she said firmly. "You didn't collect him after the third jump, you could have started him stronger and he wasn't paying attention to you every second of the course." I opened my mouth, wanting to shoot something back about how none of that was true . . . but Heather was right. Sure, it had been a strong ride, but Charm and I needed more practice before we really deserved the nines Callie and Julia had given us.

"All right," Mr. Conner said. "This was a good exercise. Hand off your horses to Mike and Doug. They'll cool and groom them after morning lessons so you can get to class on time, but they're yours in the afternoon. See you later."

The Trio dismounted and headed for the door.

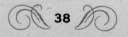

"So mature, Heather," Callie called after her. "You went after me on purpose."

"Please, Callie." Heather led Aristocrat toward the door without a glance. "You'd know it if I went after you."

"Oh, my God," Callie hissed the second the Trio was out of the arena. "She's gonna be like this all semester!"

I dismounted and urged Charm forward. "It's still better than last year. At least she's not trying to run me out of here or break up our friendship."

"True," Callie said with a sigh. "I just want to work really hard for regionals. Want to practice together on weekends?"

"Definitely. Saturday *and* Sunday, if we can. See you at English?"

"Deal!" Callie said. We gave Black Jack and Charm to Mike and Doug. It was almost eight—only twenty minutes to shower and get to class.

I hurried out of the stable and walked down the sidewalk. Ahead of me, the Trio sauntered up the path. Lateness obviously wasn't important to them.

". . . so for the Sweetheart Soirée," Heather said. "You have to remember that—"

I'd completely forgotten to ask Paige about the

mysterious Sweetheart Soirée. I walked a little closer to the Trio. Maybe I'd finally find out what—suddenly, Heather spun around and narrowed her eyes at me. Julia and Alison stopped beside her.

My face reddened and I looked down.

"Go away, Harriet the Spy!" Heather spat.

I hurried past them, not wanting to make myself even later by getting into it with Heather.

Sasha the Spy. That could be my new IM name.

5

HEATHER'S SOUR PUNCH

IT WAS FINALLY LUNCHTIME AND THE SMELLS of pizza and brownies filled the caf. English, algebra, and bio had dragged. It was our first day back, so there wasn't really much work to do, but that wouldn't last long. I slid my tray onto the table and took a seat with Paige, Callie, and Nicole.

"Status?" Paige asked me.

"Tired," I moaned. "Working out with Charm in the morning is harder than I thought. Plus, I've got another lesson after school." It was only day one and I was already complaining. I felt bad—a million students would kill to be at Canterwood and here I was complaining about it.

"It'll get easier," Paige said, poking at her strawberry

yogurt. "You've got to adjust to your new schedule."

"I guess," I said. "At least I've got film next."

"Oooh," Paige made a kissy face. "you mean your class with Jaaay-cob?"

I laughed and punched her on the arm. "Stop it!" I squealed—but I couldn't help scanning the caf for him. It was already lunchtime and I had yet to see him even once—I hadn't even passed him in between classes!

"Soon you'll ditch me and take Jacob trail riding instead," Callie teased.

"Ignore them!" Nicole said with a laugh. "They're just jealous." Nicole was on the intermediate team. Last semester, she had tried out for the advanced team but hadn't made it. She'd been crushed, but she was working hard and would definitely be trying out next fall.

At the end of the period, I got up to throw away my trash. I passed one of the long tables in the center of the room and saw the new guy, Eric, sitting with a couple of guys from Blackwell Hall. He jumped up from his table and grabbed his tray when he saw me.

"Headed to class?" he asked.

"Yeah, film," I said as we emptied our trays. "How's the first day?"

"Good so far," he said with a nod. "Except I have an

appointment with . . ." He checked his schedule. "Ms. Utz. Know where she is?"

"Yep, I'll show you. You're going to have fun with her," I laughed.

"Uh-oh," Eric looked at me skeptically. "Why?"

I bit my lip as we headed outside. "Let's just say she's not shy."

"Is she crazy?" he groaned.

"You have nooo idea."

"Tell me! It's just cruel to send a guy in unprepared."

"Well," I said. "Let's see. First rule—no direct eye contact."

Eric's eyes widened. *"What?"*

"Yeah."

"What else?" Eric asked, seeming amused.

"She wrestles," I said.

Eric stopped walking and turned to stare at me. "I can't tell if you're kidding or not," he said. "Please be kidding."

"Sorry, Eric. I'm not," I said. "She's got, like, a championship ring."

I stopped in front of Ms.Utz's office and motioned to the little reception area just inside where a couple of other students were seated and waiting.

Eric looked inside. "Okay," he said. "At least I'm not alone, right?"

"It's sort of a rite of passage," I agreed. "Good luck."

"Thanks, Sasha—I'll catch up with you later." He walked backward through into the reception area with wide eyes, with the classic mock–horror movie look that said: "If I don't make it out, call for help."

I laughed and headed for the Canterwood Media Center. Last semester, film had been an evening class on Fridays, but now the class had been moved to early Monday afternoons. I ran my fingers through my hair and applied a new coat of lip gloss as I got closer. Mint was always my go-to gloss after meals.

Jacob, hi, I practiced in my head. *You look great.*

No—way too boring. *Hey, Jacob—what's up?*

Okay, generic much? Maybe it should be more like, *Jacob! I'm so excited to see you! I've been thinking about you all break, ever since we danced at the winter dance. Are we going out, technically? Because all of my friends are asking me and I don't know how to answer them.*

Yeah, that won't freak him out at all. Not even a little bit.

No time to think now. I pushed open the door and walked inside.

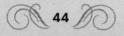

The concessions stand was closed until the theater opened tonight. I missed the smell of popcorn and the zillions of candy choices.

I was about to step into the theater when a familiar laugh made me turn around. Heather, looking stylish and pretty in a bubblegum pink puffy coat and white cashmere sweater, had her blue eyes glued to Jacob. He stood a couple of feet away from her and she twisted her bar stool back and forth. I took a deep breath and walked over. "Hi, Jacob!" I said.

"Hey, Sash!" Jacob said. He smiled at me and, I swear, subzero air radiated off Heather. "It's great to see you *finally*! Sorry we could never meet up before."

I smiled at him—this was going way better than I'd expected!

"You two have class together?" Heather snipped.

"Yeah," I said. "We sit together. Too bad you didn't sign up for film."

"There's always next semester," Heather said.

"Ugh," Jacob said. "Don't even talk about that. I need to get through this one first."

I smiled at him and inched closer. "Well," I said. "Don't want to be late."

Heather looked at her phone. "Yeah. You wouldn't want *that*."

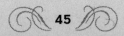

45

I half-rolled my eyes.

"See you later," Jacob said, smiling at Heather

"Later," Heather said. Her tone was sweet as strawberry Skittles, but the look she gave me when Jacob turned around was a Sour Punch.

"How was break?" I asked, ignoring her and walking with Jacob into the theater.

"It was great! My aunt and uncle came over and we played snow football on Christmas Eve."

"That sounds really fun," I said. "Snow football?"

We maneuvered down the backpack-littered main aisle to our seats.

Jacob smiled and I could see his dimples. "It's way better than playing on the grass."

My annoyance at Heather started to slip away. Talking to Jacob always made me smile.

When we reached our row, I stopped to let Jacob go first and he halted at the same time.

"You go," we said in unison. We laughed and my cheeks flushed.

Jacob motioned for me to go ahead and I did the same, mirroring him.

"I'll just go, then!" I said.

"I was about to get a traffic cop," Jacob said. He

followed me and slid into the cushy seat next to me. Maybe he didn't forget about me over break. There was a definite *like* vibe.

I wanted to ask Jacob *why* he had been talking to Heather, but I couldn't. It's not like I was for sure his girlfriend or anything. Jacob could talk to other girls if he wanted. Or even go out with them. But I hoped he wouldn't want to . . . oh, God, I was *not* going to make myself crazy over something so silly!

He'd been *talking* to Heather. That's it. I settled into my seat.

Mr. Ramirez turned on the lights and stepped to the front of the classroom. "'The best kind of prize is a surprise!'"

Mr. Ramirez often started class with a film quote.

"Johnny Depp in *Charlie and the Chocolate Factory*!" I called out.

"That's right!" Mr. Ramirez said. "Excellent, Sasha. Today's surprise is that we will be discussing our exciting semester project."

"Good job with the quote," Jacob whispered.

"In a moment, we'll begin watching *Snow White and the Seven Dwarfs*, the first full-length animated film produced by Walt Disney," Mr. Ramirez said. "But before

we start the film, let's go ahead and discuss our semester project. You will be partnered up to write, shoot, and direct a two- to four-minute film. These films will be due before midwinter break and I'll view them while you're on vacation. In just a moment, I'm going to assign partners."

Ooh! I turned to Jacob to whisper to him, but Mr. Ramirez was looking in our direction. I squinted and tried to send him an ESP signal, but he didn't look at me. Guess my powers weren't fully formed. I moved my foot to nudge the side of his seat to get this attention, but my foot slipped and kicked Jacob's leg accidentally.

"Ow!" Jacob said and looked down.

OMG!

"Sorry!" I whispered.

He gave me a sideways look and rubbed his shin.

"I'll be basing partners on alphabetic pairing," Mr. Ramirez added.

Great. He couldn't have said that two seconds ago, before I kicked my crush?

"Sorry," I whispered again when Mr. Ramirez started to name partners. "I meant to kick your chair."

"Uh huh," Jacob teased. "Sure you did. Why did you want to kick my chair?"

"I . . ." I paused, feeling shy. "I was hoping we could be partners, or something—but that was before Mr. R said partners would be alphabetical."

Jacob started to reply, but Mr. Ramirez reached us before he could.

"Sasha Silver," Mr. Ramirez called. "You'll be paired with . . . Jacob Schwartz." Yes!

Jacob grinned. "No bruises necessary."

Mr. Ramirez finished pairing everyone up. "After we watch *Snow White*, I'll hand out the genres. Each team will be assigned a genre, such as fantasy or comedy, and you may use that any way you choose."

Mr. Ramirez went to turn on the movie and Jacob leaned over to me. "Have you ever written a script before?" he asked.

"Never," I admitted, "But I'm taking creative writing this semester, so maybe that'll help."

"Cool," Jacob nodded.

We settled into our seats to watch the movie—but there was no way I could concentrate on a wicked witch and forest animals when I had just been pretty much *assigned* to spend massive amounts of time with a boy. *The* boy.

At the end of the movie, Mr. Ramirez started to pass out the genres. "Remember to read two chapters in your film textbook," he said.

I wrote down the assignment.

"Jacob and Sasha," Mr. Ramirez said. He smiled at us. "Your genre is documentary."

"Documentary," Jacob said to me. "We can do this, right?"

"We can *so* do this," I replied. "Did you see *March of the Penguins*? Maybe we could do something like that."

"That would be fun," Jacob said. "How about *Charge of the Connecticut Carpenter Ants*?"

"Aw, you stole my idea."

We laughed and started to pack up our books. Jacob shifted in his seat.

"Want to IM about ideas later?" he asked.

"It's a . . . plan."

More dimples.

In that moment, I knew there was nothing to worry about. Jacob didn't like Heather. He liked me.

6

SWEETHEART SOIRÉE SECRETS

FILM CLASS HAD ENDED HOURS AGO, BUT I kept replaying my conversations with Jacob in my head. He was definitely the cutest guy I'd ever seen. Those green-gold-flecked eyes, that hair, and . . .

"Earth to Sasha," Paige teased from her desk. "You okay?"

"Fine," I said. "Just trying to decide what Jacob and I should do for our documentary."

"It has to be good if it's worth a big part of your grade." Paige put down her butterfly-covered pencil. "Any ideas?"

"We talked about maybe something with animals. Ooh, hey—before I forget—do you know anything about this Sweetheart Soirée thing people have been talking about?"

"Not much." Paige frowned. "It's a secret. I know the

Canterwood ballroom is always the location and they bring in caterers and decorators. The Soirée is a Canterwood tradition that started back in the early eighteen eighties."

"Wow. I can't even imagine Canterwood back then," I said.

"I know. It was an all girls' school, so the guys came to the Soirée from the Dover School for Boys. There's a legend about the first Canterwood Sweetheart Soirée, too."

I sat up straighter. "Tell me!"

"Okay. So, it was, like, 1884 and the Canterwood adults decided to throw a Valentine's Day party for the staff. They thought Valentine's Day was too mature for kids."

I nodded.

"The ninth-grade girls decided to protest," Paige continued. "They sent letters to the guys at Dover and asked them to help. On the night of the party, the guys sneaked over from Dover. Everyone dressed up in their best clothes and crashed the adults' party."

"And they weren't expelled?" I asked.

"You'd think, but they weren't. The Dover boys were banned from visiting campus for the rest of the year. But the kids found a way to hold their own secret Valentine's Day party the next year. The students held it every year

until the teachers finally caught on and authorized the party in the early 1900s. But the year of separation between the guys and girls is the real legend. It's rumored that their broken hearts inspired some sort of party game that everyone still plays every year."

"Hmm," I said. "Who gets invited?"

"Everyone, I think," Paige said. "Headmistress Drake wouldn't okay a party if any of the students were excluded. I heard a rumor that last year, Canterwood hired a DJ from New York City. There was also a black tie dress code."

"Whoa." My wardrobe would need serious updating if those were the rules this year. I stretched my arms to the ceiling and yawned. "I'll have to keep trailing Heather to see if she knows more details."

Paige rolled her eyes. "She probably does know something."

"Ugh. I can't keep wasting time on her. I've got to figure out this film thing."

We were quiet for a couple of minutes and then I started thinking aloud again.

Paige ambled over to the window and looked outside. "Maybe you could film a herd of deer or . . ." She turned away from the glass and looked at me. "What animal is on campus right now?"

"Umm . . . birds?" I asked hesitantly.

Paige smacked her forehead. "Sasha Silver! C'mon!"

What other animal . . . oh! "Horses! Oh, my God, that's perfect! You're a genius!"

"Obviously," Paige said and went back to her algebra homework.

I logged into MSN and started typing a message for Jacob to get when he logged on. *i've got an idea!* I started to write when his gray offline icon turned green.

GamerGuy: hey!

SassySilver: hi! i was just leaving u an IM.

GamerGuy: yeah? did u come up w/ an idea 4 film?

SassySilver: paige did

GamerGuy: tell me. can't think of nething! :/

SassySilver: well, the only animals on campus r the horses. maybe we can do r doc on them?

While I waited a few seconds for his response, I wished I could take it back. He probably hated the idea.

GamerGuy: u know the horses rlly well, so . . . i think it's a gr8 idea.

SassySilver: u do? rlly?!

GamerGuy: we can talk 2mrw or something and come up w/ r topic. ok?

SassySilver: gr8.

GamerGuy: cul! Ttyl . . .

I logged out and looked over at Paige. "He loved your idea!"

"He did? Really?" Paige had a teal sticky note stuck to her arm. "That's great! Now you'll get to impress him even more with your horsiness."

"Right." I laughed. "I will." I flipped open my homework notebook and scanned tonight's assignments. Last semester's homework had been nothing compared to this. Biology needed to be done first since it took me the longest. Ms. Peterson had already announced that we'd have a quiz this week. I stared at the book and tried not to think about Heather and Jacob. My e-mail notifier dinged.

Hey Sasha, hope it's okay that I looked you up in the student directory. Thanks for the help today! You were right—I'll never be the same after my Utz encounter. —Eric Rodriguez

I smiled at the message before turning back to my homework. Suddenly, the work didn't seem so bad.

7

QUIZ ME

ON WEDNESDAY AFTERNOON, I HEADED TO MY usual spot in the caf—a round table under a giant window that overlooked a frozen-over grassy knoll with a stone bench.

"Sit," Paige instructed. She was sitting next to Callie and Nicole and they were sharing a giant plate of curly fries.

"Can't," I said.

"Why?" Callie asked. She put down her fry.

"I have a bio quiz today," I said. "I've got to study."

"Want help?" Paige asked.

"No, it's okay." I adjusted the backpack strap that started to dig into my shoulder. "I'm just going to sit over there and study."

"Yell if you want help," Nicole said.

"I will."

Sigh. I didn't want to sit by myself. I'd much rather sit with Paige, Callie, and Nicole and gossip about our day. I walked over to a tiny table with two chairs by one of the windows. The table was barely big enough for my bio book and tray. I popped open my Sprite and flipped to chapter three. My grades were too important to slack off now. Especially with regionals coming up.

I tried to force down my panic and concentrate, but nerves didn't help.

My phone buzzed. It was Jacob.

Hey S—I got an idea 4 film.

What? I texted back.

How about the intelligence of horses. U always say Charm is smart. Can U prove it on camera?

Definitely! I texted.

That was a good topic, but I'd have to think of a way to show how smart Charm was. I redirected my obsessive focus to bio. For now, this was my main priority.

I read the first paragraph three times until it finally sank in and then I started on the rest of the text. My queasy stomach told me this wasn't going to be enough studying.

Twenty minutes later, I looked over at Paige and Callie's table and saw they were already gone. I dumped my tray, slid my backpack over my shoulder, and picked up my book. I could get in a few extra seconds of studying while I walked to class. I headed across the caf, keeping one eye in front of me and one on my book.

"Hey."

Eric stood in from of me, wearing a black jacket over a green polo shirt and slouchy cargo pants.

"On your way to class?" I asked.

"PE," he said. "Ms. Yee is teaching us how to play squash. What about you?"

I held up my book and made a face. "Bio. I've got a quiz that I'm totally going to fail."

"Uh-oh. Want me to quiz you on the way over? The gym's on the way."

"Oh." I paused for a second. "No, that's okay. I don't want you to be late or anything."

He shook his head. "Bio is my best subject."

Well, if he was going to insist . . .

"Okay." I handed him the book. "Ask me anything."

He scanned the page. "How many bones are in an adult body?"

I thought for a second. "Two hundred and six?"

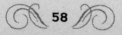

"That's right! Okay, question two."

By the time we reached my classroom, Eric had asked me twenty questions and I'd only messed up a few.

"I'm sure you'll do fine," he said. He pushed his dark hair out of his eyes and handed me the book.

"Thanks to you," I said. "Are you riding later?"

"Yeah, you?"

"I'll see you there."

"Good—see you there." Eric turned and headed out the door to go to gym.

I watched him walk away and crossed my fingers. Even with Eric's help, it was going to take a miracle to get a good grade.

8

ALL FOR ONE, AND ONE FOR ALL. NOT.

CANTERWOOD TEACHERS MUST HAVE TAKEN a course over break on how to torture their students. If we didn't have homework, we had papers or pop quizzes. I knew they were trying to prep us for finals, but it was only the first week back to school!

Saturday had finally come.

"You riding today?" Paige asked, flipping through *Martha Stewart Living*.

"Yeah, but I've got to send an e-mail with the film proposal to Mr. Ramirez. He wanted them *yesterday*, but Jacob and I couldn't decide on one until this morning."

"What'd you pick?" Paige closed the magazine and peered at my laptop screen where I had my e-mail open.

"We decided to do it about how horses are smarter than people think."

"How're you going to do that?" Paige pulled on her pink snow boots.

"Well, we don't know yet. I'm still thinking!" I watched Paige head for the door. "Where are you going?"

"My friend Erin, in Orchard Hall, has a strawberry tart recipe she thinks I should consider for my application. Then I'm going to write the first draft of my essay for my contest packet."

"I'll come with you to Orchard," I said. "I've got to meet Callie before we ride."

I sent off my e-mail to Mr. Ramirez, and then pulled on a stable jacket, one with a few stubborn stains from Charm's grassy mouth, and tugged on my boots.

Paige and I got halfway down the hallway when a hot pink flyer shaped like a rose caught our attention.

"It's another Sweetheart Soirée announcement!" Paige said.

We hurried over to the bulletin board.

THE SWEETHEART SOIRÉE MAY BE FAR AWAY,

BUT KEEP YOUR EYES HERE . . . FOR ATTENTION YOU MUST PAY.

MORE FLYERS WILL COME, SO LOOK FOR ANOTHER RHYME.

IF YOU DON'T PAY HEED,

YOU'LL SOON BE OUT OF TIME.

"Wow," Paige whispered. "This is going to be so fun! I can't wait."

"Me neither," I agreed. "I have a feeling it's going to be *huge!*"

We looked at each other for a second before we headed back down the hallway and walked across campus. I hunched against the cold. Our shoes crunched over the brown grass.

Orchard, a stark contrast from Winchester, had beige-and-cranberry-colored walls. The old, wooden floors were shiny and polished. I loosened my coat and enjoyed the toasty warmth. I headed for Callie's room on the second floor and Paige went up another floor to find her recipe. I paused by the glass door that overlooked a small balcony. I could just see the stable roof from here.

I knocked on Callie's white door, covered with "Canterwood Crest is the best!" stickers. Callie, dressed in her breeches and a purple hoodie that set off her dark hair and honey-colored eyes, pulled open the door. "Sasha!"

"I walked over with Paige," I explained. "She came to

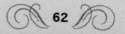

get a recipe from some girl named Erin, so I thought I'd tag along and meet you a little early."

Callie nodded and pulled her black hair into a pony-tail. "Yeah, Erin is the recipe girl of Orchard."

I sat on Callie's desk chair and looked around. I'd only been in her dorm a few times last semester, and not once since school had started again.

Grand Prix and Olympic posters with world-class equestrians covered Callie's side of the room. Her plum-colored bedspread stood out against the dark, polished wood floors. Pictures of her little brothers and parents sat on her desk in funky-shaped frames.

"Ready?" Callie asked.

"Ready," I said.

We headed out the door. "What do you want to work on today?"

"Well, I was thinking Jack's stride is a little short and—" Callie stopped when we passed Orchard's common room.

"I know, Dad. I know." Heather's voice came from inside.

Callie and I hung back, hugging the wall. I peered inside carefully. Heather was perched on the edge of one of one of the room's recliners and she held her phone five inches away from her ear. A math textbook, crumpled papers, and pens littered the table.

"Dad, you don't have to worry," Heather said. Her free hand clenched into a fist. "My riding *will* be enough to get me through regionals. I don't have to cheat!"

My eyes widened. Callie gripped my arm.

"Dad," Heather sighed, digging her toes into the carpet. "I'm the best on the team. I'll win my classes. We still have weeks to practice and—"

Mr. Fox must have cut her off because she stopped talking.

Heather stood and started to pace. "Dad! You can't bribe a judge! I'll win on my own."

She looked as if she was going to toss the phone across the room. She swallowed hard and her face reddened. "If you do that, I'm not going to regionals. I'll tell Mr. Conner that I'm sick."

I shifted in the hallway and my boot squeaked. Heather's head snapped in our direction. *Run!* shot through my brain. Callie and I shot off down the hallway and hid around the corner. For a minute, we couldn't hear anything. When we were sure Heather hadn't followed us, we went to the front door and slipped out of Orchard.

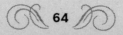

Once we were out of sight, I stopped and put my hands on my hips. "What was *that*?"

"You know Mr. Fox," Callie said. "He'll do whatever it takes to make Heather win. He wants her on the YENT."

"Yeah, but bribing a judge? C'mon, that's crazy, even for him. If he got caught, Heather's riding career would be over."

Callie shrugged. "It's worth the risk to some people. But you heard Heather—she won't do it."

"What if she changes her mind?"

"No way." Callie shook her head. "I've known her longer than you have. She's not like that. She loves to win, but she wants to do it herself. She's too competitive to win like that."

"Too bad she doesn't want the *whole* team to do well," I grumbled as we reached the stable yard.

"I guess," Callie said.

"You guess?"

Callie got quiet for a second and adjusted her fuzzy ear warmers. "I mean, yeah, we do have to ride as a team, but during a show, you're on your own."

I blinked and glanced at Callie as we walked over the frozen ground. I hadn't expected her to say that. Callie was usually the cheerleader for teamwork.

65

"Sasha, you know how it is. Sure, people look at Canterwood as a whole, but scouts don't pick entire teams for the YENT. They take single riders—individuals. They'd never choose everyone on the Canterwood team."

"No, I'm sure they wouldn't, but you can't ride just for yourself. Mr. Conner keeps saying we have to help the team."

Our boots crunched over the icy grass and I dabbed a bit of lemon gloss on my lips just to give my hands something to do. Even though we'd only been friends for six months, I thought I'd known Callie pretty well—maybe I didn't know her as well as I'd thought.

"I'll do everything I can for the team, you know that," Callie said. "But if I have to do something more—something better—to get scouts to notice me, I will. And so will Heather. And so should you."

9

A-GIRL TO F-GIRL

A GIANT RED F WAS SLASHED ACROSS MY biology quiz. *Sasha, see me after class* was scrawled next to it.

An F. Not a C or even a D, but an actual F. My face reddened. Not a good way to start a Monday.

In front of me, Julia and Alison turned around to see my quiz. I flipped over the paper, but it was too late. Julia gave me a stony glare and shook her head. The Canterwood team needed me at regionals. I kept my eyes on my desk and refused to look at anyone.

Ms. Peterson dismissed the class and I hung back in my seat, pretending to pick up all of my papers slowly, as everyone else shuffled outside. I didn't want anyone to know why I was staying behind.

"Um, Ms. Peterson?" I stepped up to her desk and clutched the quiz in my hand.

"Yes, Sasha. Thanks for staying over for a minute." Ms. Peterson adjusted her rimless glasses and closed her grade book.

"I'm sorry about the quiz. I studied hard." *But it wasn't enough*, I thought.

Ms. Peterson nodded. "I know you did. You came close on many of the answers, but I don't think you understand the material."

My face burned. This had *never* happened at Union. I had gone from A-girl to failure in months. What if I didn't make honor roll again? I had made it every single time at Union. That had been my thing—the stable girl who always made high honors.

"I'd like to see you get some help. Would you like me to set you up with one of my older students? There are several high school seniors in my advanced classes who tutor."

No way was some random stranger going to find out how dumb I was. Plus, doing biology in front of a science whiz would make me nervous. What if I kept getting the answers wrong and the tutor couldn't help me? Then what?

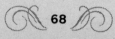

"Thanks, but I'll try to study on my own a little more first."

Ms. Peterson took off her glasses. "Don't be afraid to ask for help, Sasha. This is difficult material. You're a smart girl. I know you can do this, but if you want to stay after and have me help you with your homework, just let me know."

"Okay. Thanks."

I couldn't wait to get out of here. "Sasha?" Ms. Peterson called. "I'm sorry, but if you fail another quiz, I will have to call your parents. Canterwood policy."

Oh, great. Just great. I nodded and slid out the door. That could NOT happen! It was only the second week of school and I'd already failed something. My grades had to be good or no show for me and Charm. I jammed the paper into my backpack.

Callie was waiting for me around the corner.

"What's wrong?" she asked, getting a glimpse of my face.

"Failed a quiz," I mumbled, applying a sticky layer of strawberry shortcake lip gloss—perfect for a crisis.

"It's just one quiz. You'll do better on the next one!"

"I have to. Or my grade will be too low to show at regionals."

"Don't worry about it," Callie said. "You can do it."

I smiled at her and wondered how I'd ever felt weird around her after she'd made the comments about the show. Callie was competitive—there was nothing wrong with that. But when I needed her, she was there for me.

We linked arms and ambled out of the building. Seeing Charm would definitely make me feel better.

Inside the stable, Callie and I headed for Charm's and Black Jack's stalls.

"Let's take them for a walk before the meeting," Callie said. "Since we don't have time to ride today." Mr. Conner had sent the seventh grade advanced team e-mails yesterday and had announced today's unmounted meeting.

"Okay." I grabbed Charm's lead line off the hook outside his stall. "Hey, handsome." Charm's ears pricked forward and he came right to the stall door. One look at Charm's big brown eyes made my worry fade a little. *It's just one quiz.* I repeated Callie's words from earlier. "Let's focus on you, mister."

Charm snorted and gave me a look that said, *Of course you will.* I pulled open his stall door and clipped the lead line onto his halter.

Charm and I met Callie and Black Jack by the hot

walker. "Let's just walk around inside for a few minutes," Callie said. "It's way too cold outside!"

Charm followed me next to Callie and Jack. "What do you think the meeting is about?"

Callie shrugged. "I don't know. Maybe something about the show?"

Callie, Charm, Jack, and I walked slowly down the aisles. I looked at each of the horses inside the stalls. Most were geldings and mares, but there was a young stallion, Lexington, at the end box stall that Mr. Conner was training. None of us could go inside his stall because he was temperamental sometimes. I peered inside as we walked by. Lexington, a light gray, slept with one hoof cocked. Maybe next year, I'd be able to convince Mr. Conner to let me help him train a new young horse.

"Right," I said to Charm. Before I could lead him, he turned right at the end of the aisle.

"Whoa." Callie's eyes widened and she turned Black Jack so he'd follow Charm. "When did you teach him that?"

"The voice commands?" I slowed Charm's walk. "I've been working with him on those for a while. He can turn right, left, stop, and even count to five."

Callie's jaw dropped. "No way! Show me the counting! I can't even picture it."

"Okay." I halted Charm in the deserted aisle and Callie stopped Black Jack a few feet away. "Okay, Charm, let's show you off." Charm blinked his eyes in understanding and stood ready for a command.

Callie stood still and Jack seemed to watch Charm with curious eyes.

"Charm," I said, standing in front of him. Our eyes met and I lowered my voice into a commanding tone. "Three."

Charm dipped his head and then raised his left foreleg in the air. He brought it to the ground one, two, and then three times. "Yes! Good boy!" I took a sugar cube from my pocket and put it on my outstretched palm. Charm inhaled it and crunched.

"Wow!" Callie shook her head. "I can't believe you taught him that. I've only seen horses on TV do it! That's so cool."

"He loves it and—" Wait. Horses on TV. "This is it!" I shrieked. Black Jack raised his head in alarm. "My documentary topic with Jacob. We can film Charm's tricks and prove horses are smart."

"It's perfect," Callie said. "You've got to call Jacob."

"I'll call him after the meeting." Since Jacob didn't know anything about horses, it had been my job to come

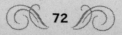

up with the perfect footage. But until today, I hadn't even thought of anything interesting. Now, I had the perfect idea and Jacob and I would be able to hang out and work with the horses.

We took Charm and Black Jack for a few more laps around the stable before we put them in their stalls. "Bye, boy," I told Charm. "You're going to be a big screen star soon!" Charm tossed his head, his forelock falling over one eye, and looked like a movie star posing on the red carpet for her latest flick. My horse was über-glam.

Callie and I met up in the skybox overlooking the arena. Mr. Conner used the smaller space when he wasn't meeting with many students.

Julia and Alison walked in and took a couple of seats behind us. They were both chomping noisily on florescent green gum. I could smell the mint from where I sat.

"Hey, guys," Callie said. She turned around and looked at them.

"Hey," Julia and Alison said together. They both wore striped sweaters over black breeches with suede knees.

Julia turned back to Alison. "Did you figure out Sunstruck's problem yet?" Julia asked.

Alison shook her head. I shifted in my seat to listen. "He won't stop cribbing! Mr. Conner and I have tried everything. We painted the door with peppery paste and sprayed it with this no-chew stuff from Horse Supply. I put a cribbing strap on him last week and it didn't even work."

"That's dangerous, too," I said. "Those pieces of wood he's swallowing could make him sick."

Alison frowned. "I know. And I'd die if something happened to him."

"Have you tried another flavor of the no-chew spray?" Callie asked. "Some horses don't mind the pepper taste."

"I've tried every flavor," Alison said. "I even did a homemade one with cayenne pepper. But he's ignoring it and chewing through the top of the stall door."

I'd just read something about cribbing in *Young Rider* last week. "He's at the end of the aisle, right?"

"Yeah." Alison nodded. "So?"

"Well, it's quiet and there's not much traffic down there. Didn't you just move him after we got back from break?"

"I did!" Alison said. "He didn't crib in his old stall. Do you think he's bored?"

"He could be," I said. "Maybe he needs to be around more people or horses. Move him or give him a stall ball."

Alison looked back and forth between Julia and me.

"I never would have thought of that," Alison said. "I'm going to move him after the meeting."

"Tell me how he does," I said.

Julia gave me a fleeting glare before looking at Alison.

"I will," Alison promised. She leaned back in her chair with a satisfied grin. The door opened and Heather stepped inside. Our smiles disappeared when Heather folded her arms and eyed us.

"What's going on?" she asked. She wedged her way between Julia and Alison, forcing Julia to move over so she could sit between them.

"Sasha gave me an idea about Sunstruck," Alison said, oblivious to Heather's death stare. "I think it might just solve his cribbing problem."

Heather pressed her lips together. "Oh." She paused. "Good. I know you were worried about that."

"I was," Alison said. "After the meeting, I'm moving him to another stall and giving him a ball to play with."

Heather nodded, but didn't say a word.

The skybox door opened again and Mr. Conner stepped inside. He pulled off his black gloves and tousled the snow out of his hair. "Hi, girls," he said. He pulled up a chair and plopped his paperwork on the desk. "We've got a few regionals things to talk about."

"Yes!" Callie whispered. "Show study sheets!"

That made me sit up a little straighter. There wasn't much time to practice. Especially when I had to put more hours into biology. And film class. And English.

Basically everything.

Mr. Conner handed me a stack of papers. I took one and passed the stack to Callie. The heading on the paper read JUNIOR EQUESTRIAN REGIONALS RULEBOOK and it was at least two hundred bound pages of show regulations, schedules, practice suggestions, and required attire.

"And here's your parental permission form," Mr. Conner said. He handed me the next stack of papers.

Mr. Conner waited for us to stop shuffling papers before he spoke again. "Did you get the e-mail with the group practice times?"

We all nodded. The e-mail had been in my inbox last night.

Mr. Conner stood and smiled. "All right. I expect you to read the handbook several times and come to me with any questions. See you at your next practice."

I moved to get up and my foot kicked something. I looked down and saw Heather's oversize bag. A piece of notebook paper stuck out of the side pocket. Heather was still talking to Julia and Alison, so I leaned forward and

squinted at the paper. "GamerGuy" was written on the corner. In Jacob's handwriting.

I sat back in my chair. He'd given her his IM name? Why?!

Heather reached backward and snatched the bag off the floor without even looking at me.

I opened my mouth to say something, but nothing came out. She didn't need to know I'd seen that paper. She'd rub my face in it. If something was going on, Jacob would have told me.

Wouldn't he?

The Trio flounced out of the room and I took a few deep breaths before getting up.

"Want to read the rulebook together tomorrow after class?" Callie asked.

"Um, sure," I said. "I'll call you later."

I hurried away before Callie could realize something was wrong. Outside, I headed for Winchester. The air was uncomfortably cold.

"Sasha!"

Eric hurried up the sidewalk. He stepped up to me and pushed his blue hood off his head.

"Hey," I said. "Ready to run screaming out of Canterwood yet?"

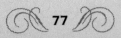

Eric laughed and we started to walk together. "After writing two papers this week, almost. But I love riding here."

"Me too," I admitted. "It makes up for the insanely tough classes."

Eric's brown eyes warmed. "Definitely. I'm riding one of Mr. Conner's school horses, Luna, and she's great."

I nodded. "I've seen other people ride her and she looks like a smooth horse."

We walked in silence for a few seconds. I couldn't keep my mind on our conversation. WHY did Heather have Jacob's IM name in her bag?

"Sasha?" Eric interrupted my thoughts.

"Huh? Oh, sorry," I said.

"I was just asking you if maybe I could have your number. You know . . . in case I want to text you or something."

"Oh," I said. "Sure."

He handed me his phone and I punched in my number. I gave him mine and he did the same.

We reached a fork in the sidewalk. Winchester was right and Blackwell was left.

"Bye," I said, giving him a distracted smile.

"Bye," he echoed.

When I got back to my dorm, it was empty and a sticky note was in the middle of my mirror.

Sash—I'm at cooking class. Will you please read my essay draft?
<3, P.

I sighed and pulled off my coat and boots. I sat at my desk and tried to read, but I couldn't focus.

Get a grip, I told myself.

But Heather's piece of paper kept popping into my head.

10

CHARM GETS
SCHOOLED . . .
BY HEATHER

LEAVING HEATHER AND ME ALONE TO PRACTICE
sounded like the dumbest idea Mr. Conner ever had. But
it was actually working out.

Heather and I been riding for half an hour on a freezing Wednesday afternoon and we hadn't fought once
about the lesson. We both took riding too seriously to
ruin practice with fighting. That kept me from throwing a
zillion questions at her about her "friendship" with Jacob.
Paige and I had run though every scenario about why Jacob
was hanging out with Heather.

Paige was sure they had a class together and that was
how they knew each other. After class, I was going to sneak
a couple of questions about Jacob into our conversation.

"All right," Heather said. She pulled Aristocrat up

beside me. "That's half an hour of flat work. Ready for jumping?"

"Definitely," I said. Beneath me, Charm's body tensed when he got within a few yards of Aristocrat. "It's okay," I whispered to him. "You're a better jumper than he is." Charm snorted and nodded. I hid my grin.

"Let's take those jumps," Heather said. She nodded in the direction of two verticals and a double oxer.

"Okay," I said. "You want to go first?"

"Sure." Heather flicked a bit of hay off her hunter green sweater. I looked down at my own stable coat—covered in chestnut horse hair—and tried to brush off a few.

She let Aristocrat out into a smooth canter and they circled twice before heading to the first vertical. Mr. Conner had set up three jumps that he trusted us to get over easily while he wasn't supervising. But he had repeated the "no jumping without a partner—ever!" rule about fifty times. I relaxed the reins and leaned back in the saddle, resting my hand on top of Charm's rump.

Aristocrat snapped his knees under his gleaming body and lifted into the air. He barely made a sound as he hit the ground and cantered toward the next jump. Heather gathered him and did a half halt to slow his stride before he floated over the red and white rails. They made a sweeping turn for eight or nine strides and then lined up for the double oxer. Heather's eyes centered on the jump and Aristocrat took it without hesitation. If Mr. Fox had seen that ride, he would have known Heather didn't need to bribe a judge to win.

"Nice," I called as Heather trotted Aristocrat over.

"Thanks," she said. "Your turn."

"Let's do it," I whispered to Charm. He craned his neck around to eye me and then straightened.

We cantered around the indoor arena twice, avoiding the jumps, and then I pointed Charm at the first rail. *Three, two, and now!* I counted the strides in my head. Charm's takeoff was perfect. He righted himself on the ground and then cantered toward the second jump.

"Easy," I said. He tugged on the reins and increased his speed by a fraction. *No, no—too close to the double oxer!* I thought, but it was too late. The oxer had a two-and-a-half foot spread and Charm took off too late. His back hooves clipped the second rail and it tumbled to the ground with a thunk.

Why did that have to happen in front of Heather?!

I frowned and trotted Charm next to Aristocrat. Charm's muscles tensed and he tried to shuffle away from his rival.

"That was awful," Heather said. She dropped the reins and crossed her arms. "Do it again."

She was right. I had to end the lesson with Charm on a good note or he'd lose his confidence. I didn't say a word and turned him back to the course. I rode him up to the double oxer and dismounted to set up the knocked pole.

We flew over the first two jumps, but Charm strained toward the double oxer. "Slow down," I said in a firm voice. I checked his stride, but he ignored my hands and this time, he left the ground a half-stride too early. He knocked the rail again and I fought back a scream of frustration.

"Sasha!" Heather called from her spot on the other side of the arena. "What are you doing?"

"He keeps knocking the rail," I said through gritted teeth.

"*He's* not doing it wrong," Heather said. "You are."

"No, I'm not," I protested. "He's not listening."

"You're not giving him the right cues."

That was it. "Fine," I said. I dismounted and pulled Charm's reins over his head. I held them out to Heather. "You do it, then." Charm slowed his pace and tried to back up when he realized I was leading him to Heather.

Without a word, Heather dismounted and we swapped reins. Charm's furious glare made me realize what I'd done. My horse was in enemy hands! Charm may have had two bad rounds, but he didn't deserve that.

But it was too late. Heather had already mounted. She rode Charm in a large circle to get used to him.

I turned Aristocrat in a circle and moved him back against the wall. He stepped a couple of feet sideways and stood as far away as the reins would allow. I reached out to pet him, but he laid back his ears and watched Heather and Charm.

I'd never seen anyone else but Kim, my old instructor, ride Charm before. It killed me to watch him move fluidly (sigh) under Heather. His rounded back and arched neck looked near perfect from my spot on the sidelines.

Heather's hands softened and she urged Charm over the first jump. He didn't hesitate—he rose into the air. They cleared the second vertical without fault. Heather closed her fingers around the reins and asked Charm to slow before the double oxer. He—*my* horse!—responded to her command and he collected his stride before popping over the double. They landed just feet away from the jump and with a triumphant grin, Heather guided him over to me.

"That was nice," I admitted. I waited for Heather to dismount, but she stayed on Charm and circled him.

"You should try Aristocrat," she said. "Mr. Conner keeps telling us we should ride different horses."

True. He had said that. Most Olympic riders had two or three horses to ride in case one became injured.

"You sure?" I asked. I'd never seen anyone else ride her hundred thousand–dollar horse—not even Julia or Alison!

"It's fine," Heather said.

I turned so I couldn't see Charm's face and gathered the reins in my left hand. I slid my foot into the stirrup iron and lifted myself into the saddle. Aristocrat danced beneath me and I squeezed my legs firmly against his sides. He listened and moved forward, flicking an ear back to listen for another command.

"Good boy," I said. His good manners won out over his dislike for me.

He didn't rush the verticals and jumped them as if he could do it all day. He moved easily toward the double oxer and I sat still and gave him his head. His timing was perfect—we cleared the poles by several inches.

"All right!" Heather called from atop Charm's back.

"He's a great horse," I said. I patted Aristocrat's neck and tried to avoid looking at Charm. He strained against

the reins to reach me, but recoiled when Aristocrat blew a breath in his face.

Heather nodded. "He really is. Charm is better than I thought."

I decided to let that go.

"So," I said. "Next time we'll work on endurance and timing?"

"Sounds good. Maybe go canter up and down the hills for an hour."

"Can you make the next practice?" I asked. "Or . . . are you meeting someone or something?"

Heather frowned. "Meeting someone? Like . . . ?"

"I don't know." I paused. "Maybe Julia or Alison or a guy or . . ." I trailed off.

"Aw," she said. "You think I'm meeting Jacob. Maybe I am. What's it to you?"

"You're only interested in him because *I* like him."

"I'm just giving him options," Heather said.

"He doesn't need options. He likes *me*."

We both turned when we heard a huff from the arena door. Julia, with arms folded, frowned at us. She looked as if she was hiding in her oversize royal blue sweater that almost covered her knees. "You're letting *her* ride Aristocrat?" Julia squeaked.

Heather jutted out her chin. "She was taking a jump wrong, so I had to show her how to get over the oxer. Relax."

"But you never let anyone ride him." Julia's voice turned to a whisper as she looked at Heather. "*I've* never ridden him."

Heather gave an exaggerated sigh. "Jules, we're busy. Okay?"

Without another word, Julia spun around and left. Heather didn't move to go after her.

We dismounted and swapped reins. The horses followed us and as we circled the arena to cool them out.

"Did you ever find out more details about the Sweetheart Soirée?" Heather asked.

"Actually, I did," I said. I tried to sound as if I didn't care. "Paige told me everything."

Heather froze. "She did?"

I smiled. "Every detail."

Okay, that wasn't completely true, but I loved seeing Heather squirm!

Heather sniffed. "Whatever she told you was probably wrong anyway."

I shrugged, leading Charm forward.

Heather pulled Aristocrat beside Charm and looked at

me. "You should probably tell me what she said. Then I can tell you how wrong she is."

"Nah," I said with a grin. "You're right—it's probably wrong and you wouldn't want to hear it."

"But—" Heather started.

I held back a laugh and walked Charm away.

11

DESSERT— THE NEW FOOD GROUP

CLASSES HAD ENDED FOR THE WEEK, BUT Paige's School of Culinary Arts was in full swing. Paige and I had barricaded ourselves in the Winchester common room to make potential recipes for her application.

"Try this one," she said. She thrust a wooden spoon in my face.

"Paige," I moaned. "I've been tasting for an hour. I'm going to explode!"

"Just one more," she begged.

"One. Then I have to change and get ready to meet Callie for a trail ride."

I took the spoon and Paige watched me with hands clasped, waiting for a yes or no.

"Very good," I mumbled with a mouthful of berry. "Tangy."

"Excellent." Paige made a check mark on her pink clipboard and moved to the fridge.

Livvie poked her head in the door. She caught a glimpse of the bowls, pans, and flour containers on the counters. "You *are* cleaning this up, right?"

"The second I'm done," Paige said.

"And you know where the fire extinguisher is?" Livvie asked.

"Under the sink," Paige and I chorused.

"Homework done?"

"Livvie," Paige said. "It's Friday."

"It doesn't hurt to get an early start," Livvie said, turning away and disappearing down the hallway.

"Anyway . . ." I laughed. "What else are you going to make?"

Paige consulted her list. "Apple strudel, triple-berry pie, and butterscotch cookies."

I headed for the door. "Save me some."

When I got to the stable twenty minutes later, Nicole had her gelding, Wish, crosstied in the aisle. Troy and Andy, two guys from the intermediate team, stood with her and they were all laughing.

"Going trail riding?" Nicole asked me when I got closer.

"Yep," I said. "Callie's coming with me. You guys want to come?"

Andy groaned. "Thanks, but no. We just finished an *insane* lesson with Mr. Conner. I don't know if I'll ever ride again."

"Yeah, right," Troy said. He shook his head, but his spiky hair didn't move. "You'll be the first one at lessons on Monday—after Ben, of course. We all know why *he* gets here early."

I shrugged. "Why?"

"To see his girlfriend," Andy said. "Juuuuulia."

"What?!" I said. "No. Are you sure?"

Nicole nodded and her blond curls bounced. "They're totally going out."

"Wow," I said.

Julia and Ben. I'd seen him around before—he was pale with short black hair and arms toned from riding.

"I've got to tack up, but thanks for cluing me in!" I told Nicole.

"Anytime." She smiled and turned to Troy and Andy. "One of you guys has to carry my saddle."

I sighed. Were everyone else's relationships less complicated than mine?

*

Later, Callie and I led our horses out of the stable and into the grassy yard.

"Trail ride, ho!" Callie said. We'd gotten permission from Mr. Conner to practice cross-country as long as we stayed together and had our phones.

"Yes, we'll gallop our steeds and hunt for hounds," I added. Canterwood *did* kind of look like the English countryside with its stone walls and rolling hills. We mounted Charm and Black Jack. The two horses were on their toes. They eyed the trail ahead and broke into a trot before we even gave the signals.

"Guess they've had enough of lessons, huh?" I asked Callie.

She nodded and adjusted her padded cross-country vest. "No kidding. At least the snow is melted for now and we could get them outside to practice cross-country. Even though I'm not showing in that class, I've still got to practice."

"Didn't Mr. Conner say if we make the Youth Equestrian National Team, we can do three-day eventing?"

"Yeah," Callie said. "That means at each show, we'll have to compete in three classes—cross-country, dressage, and show jumping. If that happens, I've really got to work harder on show jumping."

I looked at Callie out of the corner of my eye.

Charm walked under a low-hanging tree branch and I leaned forward. "Charm and I will have to do more dressage. But I guess for now we'll just focus on regionals."

Callie nodded. "I'm glad I don't have many other activities this semester. Just riding and yearbook club."

"And endless studying," I said.

"How's bio?" Callie asked.

"Hard," I said. "I've got a big quiz coming up and I'm studying twenty-four/seven."

Callie gave me a sympathetic smile. "It'll get easier."

"I hope so. Okay, we talk about school too much! Want to warm them up and take a few jumps?"

"Let's go!"

Callie heeled Black Jack into a canter and Charm and I shot after her. Charm's mane, almost fully grown in since he'd doubled as Aristocrat's chew toy last fall, whipped against my arms. His gait was smooth and even. We powered forward and Charm and Jack playfully challenged each other to see who could keep his nose in front of the other. Callie and I looked at each other for a quick second before we split around a maple tree and let the horses quicken their canter. This was the best way to spend a Saturday! Sunlight streamed through the trees and helped keep off

the winter chill. Charm relaxed beneath me—I could feel his muscles warming up.

Callie and I slowed Jack and Charm to a walk. We wandered into the middle of a large clearing. Woods surrounded us and made the jumping space private. I looked around the perimeter to check for deer. The grass was brown and dry, but the ground wasn't frozen, so we were safe to jump. "What's our jumping order?" I asked.

Callie paused and surveyed our options. "Hmm. How about taking the log first, then the brush, the creek, and finally over the gate."

"Perfect. Want to go first?"

Callie nodded and tightened the chin strap on her helmet. She turned Jack in a circle. "Let's pretend it's a real cross-country course. I'll take Jack near the clearing's opening. Yell when you want me to start."

"Okay." Charm and I walked off to the sidelines and waited for Callie and Black Jack to get into position.

I gave her a few seconds to settle him before screaming, "Go!" The second the word was out of my mouth, Jack burst into a collected canter. He moved easily over the grass and Callie guided him toward the log. He tucked his legs under him and leapt strongly over the two-foot-high log. Callie kneaded her hands along his neck and asked

him to canter faster as they swept around the outskirts of the clearing and headed for a line of brush.

Charm craned his neck to watch them. Jack didn't hesitate before the brush, and landed smoothly on the other side. I urged Charm into a trot and we stayed well behind Jack and Callie. Jack trotted down a gentle incline and the grass changed to dirt. Callie pulled Jack to a slow canter and his hooves struck the hard ground before he reached the creek bed. She leaned forward, signaling Black Jack to take off. He jumped over the frozen creek and cantered up the embankment.

Charm and I took the creek at the skinniest point and then followed Callie as Jack cantered the final strides to an old wooden gate. The fence and gate separated Canterwood's property from an old abandoned farm. Mr. Conner had said we could jump the gate as long as we didn't explore the property. Jack didn't even hesitate when he saw the gate. Callie's blue coat bunched as she leaned forward on Jack's takeoff. Jack bounded over it and Callie pulled him up on the other side.

"That was great!" I called from my side of the fence. "Perfect!"

Callie leaned down and rubbed Jack's neck. The gelding was barely winded. "Well, not perfect, but he did

a good job. He didn't even look at the creek when we took it!"

I rode Charm up to the gate and unlatched it so Jack didn't have to jump it again. Once Callie and Jack rode through, I nudged Charm forward and I latched the gate to the fencepost, locking us inside.

Callie walked Black Jack in circles while I rode Charm back a few yards and got ready to take the cross-country course backward. "You ready, boy?" I asked Charm. He nodded once and we turned to face an old red-and-white barn. My muscles tensed as I readied myself in the saddle and prepared to wheel Charm around and head for the gate.

Callie counted us down. "Three, two, one, go!" On "go," Charm whirled around and went for the gate. We were a stride away before I knew it and then his body lifted into the air. We landed roughly on the ground and I gripped the saddle tighter with my knees as Charm raised his head and found an even stride. I forgot that Callie and Black Jack were behind us and concentrated on Charm. He soared over the creek and the brush, then cantered toward the log. His hooves pounded evenly over the ground and I gave him more rein. I tensed in the saddle and almost signaled Charm to jump a second too early. *Wait*, I wanted to cry, but he already knew.

He ignored my signals and took the jump at the right time. We landed on the other side and I stayed glued to the saddle. My timing on the log was awful, but Charm did great. "Good job!" I told him. Charm slowed to a trot and I patted his neck. He danced in a semicircle, proud of the jumps he'd tackled. That would have been a better round if I hadn't tensed before the log.

"Perfect!" Callie said, as she and Jack reached our sides.

But she was wrong. *Her* ride had been perfect. Not mine.

"Yeah, but didn't you see?" I shook my head and pointed to the log jump. "I totally froze. If Charm hadn't known better, we could have slammed into the log."

Callie rode closer as we turned the horses back toward Canterwood. "But you didn't. Charm did great and you only tensed a little bit."

"But there will be tons of solid fences at regionals, so I can't mess up like that."

"You won't," Callie promised. "You'll do great."

As we meandered down the frigid trail, past bare trees and dead brush, all I could think about was that second of fear that had made me overreact when we'd approached the log.

And the worst part? I'd frozen in front of Callie.

*

Half an hour later, I was finishing Charm's cooldown when my phone buzzed in my pocket. I flipped it open and saw a text alert from a blocked number.

I opened the message and immediately felt my heart begin to pound in my chest: it was a clear photo of Heather and Jacob in the library. Heather's head was bent toward Jacob's—and her smile was unmistakable. Jacob was leaning over a book, his face just inches away from Heather's.

I slammed my phone shut and looked over my shoulder half-expecting Heather to be cackling behind me. But no one was there.

They were probably just studying, I told myself.

But I couldn't calm myself down. I was the exact opposite of cool. My fingers shook as I speed-dialed Jacob.

"Hey, Ebert," Jacob said. His friendly tone made me relax a bit.

"Hey, Roeper," I said. "Um, I was wondering if you wanted to film our project tomorrow."

"Definitely! Is ten okay?"

"Great," I said, with a sigh of relief.

"You're not a bad partner," Jacob said.

I smiled.

"You know, for a girl," he added.

My smile slipped. His tone was teasing, but it didn't feel that way. *For a girl.* Why did he say that? Unless . . . he'd wanted one of his friends to be his partner. OMG. And now he was stuck with me!

Jacob is a guy, I reminded myself after we hung up. *Guys don't want to hang out with girls twenty-four/seven.*

But no matter how hard I tried, I couldn't get the picture of Jacob and Heather out of my head—it sure seemed like he wouldn't mind hanging out with *her* twenty-four/seven.

12

STARRING . . .

THE AIR WAS FROSTY ON SATURDAY MORNING.
Outside the stable, I checked my phone again. Jacob was
only five minutes late—but still.

I looked over to the small outdoor arena. Eric was
riding Luna through figure eights. I watched as his legs
made her flea-bitten gray body bend and switch directions
with ease. His body position was perfect in tall boots and
matching helmet, black breeches, and a tan coat.

I left the stable entrance and climbed the fence to
watch. Eric was so focused on Luna that it took him a
while to notice me. He beamed at me and put the reins in
one hand to wave. He turned Luna toward me and trotted
her up to the fence.

"So what's the verdict," he said. "How bad am I?"

"What?!"

"C'mon, superstar rider. Just tell me!"

"Eric—no, you're amazing." He looked at me doubt-fully. "I'm serious. Your turns are excellent. Luna really listens so well to you."

"Thanks, Sash," he smiled. "Hey—I've got to take her through a few more exercises . . . but maybe we can trail ride together sometime?"

"Definitely," I said.

Eric touched his crop to his helmet and turned Luna away from the fence. He was one of the quietest riders I'd ever seen. The movement of his fingers was slight and his leg aids to Luna were barely visible. He guided her through a sitting trot and several laps of a smooth canter before halting her in the center and backing her straight to the fence.

"Here you are."

I turned my head and saw Jacob standing a few feet behind me.

"Hey! You have to watch this for a sec—Eric's riding so well."

Jacob stepped up and peered over the fence. "That guy?"

I nodded. Eric was *beyond* good. There was no way he wouldn't make the advanced team next year.

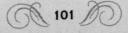

After a few more circles in the arena, Eric slowed Luna and trotted her up to us. Luna's chest was darkened with sweat that made the darker gray spots on her chest and legs stand out.

Jacob tipped his chin at Eric.

"Hey," Eric said. "I'm Eric."

"Jacob."

I waited for Jacob to say more, but he didn't. He adjusted the camera bag on his shoulder and tapped the feet of the tripod with his sneaker. A cloud passed in front of the weak sun and it cast a shadow over the arena.

Okay, so one-word responses were popular. Guess they weren't going to say anything else to each other.

"I've never been crazy about flea-bitten grays, but her coloring is great," I said to Eric.

He nodded. "I love it, too. Her coat doesn't show dirt, either."

"Don't you worry about that spreading to other horses?" Jacob asked.

Eric and I looked at him. "What?" I asked.

"The fleas," Jacob said. "Isn't that bad?"

I held back a laugh and locked eyes with Eric for a second.

"Well, there actually aren't any fleas. The color, with

all of those spots, is called that because the dots look like flea bites."

I tried to say it without making him feel stupid. It wasn't his fault he didn't know anything about horses. If he'd asked me about something he knew a lot about—like football—I would have been just as clueless.

"Oh," Jacob said. He backed away from the fence and kicked his black sneaker in the grass.

Eric shifted Luna closer to me and Jacob's jaw tightened. Jacob stood straighter and out of the corner of my eye, I watched as Eric mirrored him.

"So, you guys don't have any classes together?" I asked with forced cheerfulness. Maybe they'd seen each other in class and hadn't talked before.

"No," Eric and Jacob said at the same time.

"Maybe next year," I said.

The boys glared at each other.

"How did that bio quiz go? You know, the one I helped you with?" Eric asked.

Jacob turned to look at me.

I shook my head. "Not great. But it wasn't your fault. I should have studied more."

"*I'll* help you with the next quiz, if you need it," Jacob said.

I smiled at him. But he wasn't smiling. His eyes were on Eric. Eric stared right back.

"Uh, well, we've got to go," I told Eric. "We're doing a film project."

"Okay, I'll see you later." Eric said. "I'll be around the stable all weekend." He threw me a grin and urged Luna forward.

Jacob jumped to the side to get out of Luna's way and stood a little closer to me.

"Is he . . ." Jacob paused. " . . . on your team?"

"No," I said. "He's on the intermediate team."

"Oh," Jacob said with a half-smile.

"Ready to go?" I started to walk into the stable.

"Sure," Jacob said. He lagged behind me as we stepped inside the stable and walked down the aisle. A couple of horses were crosstied ahead of us. I ducked under the ropes and I turned to talk to Jacob, but he had stopped before the ties.

"What's wrong?" I asked.

"Nothing," he said quickly. "Are we supposed to walk around the horses like that?"

"Oh, yeah. It's fine. They're used to people doing that."

A palomino mare in crossties shook her head.

"Uh, this blond horse looks upset," Jacob said.

I hid my grin and ducked back under the crossties. "Actually, we call her a palomino. I'll hold her head. Go ahead."

Jacob shot me a grateful smile and hurried under the crossties.

"Good girl," I said, patting her neck.

I caught up to Jacob and pointed down the aisle. "Charm's stall is this way," I said. "Charm," I called to him. I unlatched the door and grabbed a lead line off the hook. Jacob stood in the aisle with his arms crossed. "This is Jacob," I said. I led Charm out of the stall and Jacob took two steps back.

He looked at Charm and nodded. "He looks nice."

Nice? Oh, God. He hated me. He wanted a different partner—anyone but me. He didn't even want to pet my horse!

"If you want, we can take him to the arena and film there. It's empty right now."

"Let's do it," Jacob said. "Which way?"

"To the right."

Before Charm and I walked two steps, Jacob was down the aisle and walking to the arena. He obviously couldn't wait to get away from me.

This was such a disaster. Disappointment burned in my throat and I tried not to cry. If he hadn't wanted to work with me, he should have told Mr. Ramirez. Something must have happened between now and yesterday when we'd talked.

I led Charm into the arena and pulled the door shut behind me. I tied Charm to the rail so I could help Jacob set up our equipment. Without looking at Jacob, I walked over to him and unzipped the camera.

"This is a great spot," Jacob said. He flashed me a smile and his green eyes stayed on my face. "I'm glad we're doing this together."

Wait. He'd ignored me and sulked for the past five minutes. Now he was happy to be my partner?

I gave him a shaky smile. "Me too." I think.

Jacob started setting up the tripod and he attached a longer lens to his camera. "So, you ride Eastern, right?"

I giggled.

"What's so funny?" Jacob turned to me and crossed his arms. An easy grin slipped over his face.

"Well, it's English or Western," I explained. "I ride English."

"No Eastern?"

"No Eastern."

We laughed. This was what it was supposed to be like. He was funny and sweet, and it was nice to be having fun again.

"I'm going to get Charm and bring him over," I said.

"Just call me Spielberg for the rest of the shoot," Jacob instructed.

I nodded and went to get Charm. Maybe Jacob had gotten up too early and had been grouchy earlier. He was acting like the old Jacob now. The one who might actually go with me to the Sweetheart Soirée. . . .

I led Charm in front of the camera and took a breath. If we were going to prove horses were smart, we couldn't reshoot if Charm didn't do the trick. That would be a total mockumentary.

"We can't rehearse the dialogue either, right?" I asked Jacob.

"Right," he said. "Just speak naturally."

"Okay." I ran my fingers through my hair and then untangled a knot in Charm's chestnut mane.

"Quiet on the set!" Jacob announced. He looked over the camera at me. "*Horse Sense*, take one. Ready and . . . action!"

I looked into the camera and started talking. "Ever wonder how smart animals *really* are?" I asked. "If you have,

then this documentary is for you. I'm Sasha, and my partner Jacob and I are going to test our theory that horses are more intelligent than people think." My eyes connected with Jacob's and he nodded for me to keep going.

I resumed my I-should-get-an-Oscar-for-this voice. "I'm going to ask my horse, Charm, to count. I've taught Charm how to count up to five and I want to prove that he can do it."

I turned my head to Charm and led him in a circle. Jacob followed our movement with the camera.

"Ready, boy?" I asked Charm. He nodded and kept one eye on me and one on the camera.

"Charm," I said in a clear voice. "Three."

Charm lowered his head and pawed the ground. I counted aloud. "One." Charm struck again. "Two." Then again. "Three! Good job!" I reached into my pocket and pulled out a chunk of carrot. Charm greedily snatched the carrot off my hand and munched while I talked.

"So, Charm has just counted to three. But to really prove my point, our director, Jacob, is also going to ask Charm to count."

Jacob's eyes met mine and I waved him over.

"Um, how do I ask him?" Jacob asked. He stood away from Charm and twisted his hands.

"Say his name and then tell him a number between one and five," I said.

Jacob cleared his throat and flashed a smile at the camera. "Charm," he said. "One."

Charm lifted his foreleg high in the air and tossed his mane for the camera. He brought his hoof down once and then looked at me expectantly. I dug into my pocket for another treat. "Good boy," I said.

Jacob let out a breath and turned to the camera. "I hope we've demonstrated that horses are smarter than people often give them credit for being. Thanks for watching and look for another film from S and S soon."

He hurried to turn off the camera.

"S and S?" I asked with a raised eyebrow.

He smiled at me in a way that made me lean on Charm for support. "Silver and Schwartz."

"Oh." I couldn't think of anything else to say. I tied Charm to the rail again. Together, Jacob and I watched the footage he had shot before we dismantled the equipment. It looked like an A-film to me.

Things were going so well . . . but one thing was still nagging me. That picture. If I . . . I had to ask him about Heather.

"Jacob?"

He put down the camera bag. "Yeah?"

"I saw you with my teammate Heather the other day and . . ." I trailed off. The words wouldn't come out. Mom had always taught me to be confident and independent—now I sounded insecure and silly.

Jacob turned to face me and behind us, Charm snorted. Or snored. Not sure.

"Heather? We have a class together," he said. He gave me a smile and a look like I was insane for thinking he liked her.

"Oh, 'cause I was just wondering," I rambled. "I didn't know if you liked her or something."

Jacob shook his head. He opened his mouth and then his phone dinged. I turned back to the camera so he could check his text.

"I've got to run," he said. "Sorry." He snapped the phone shut and shoved it in his pocket.

"Is something wrong?"

He shook his head as he put the camera bag over his shoulder. "Oh, no, everything's fine. I'll text you when I get the editing done."

"Okay," I called after him. "Bye." But he was already out the door.

"He should try out for the track team," I grumbled to myself.

I ambled over to Charm and untied his lead line. "What was that about, boy?" I whispered to him. I tried not to think about it as I put Charm away, but all I could see was the picture of Jacob and Heather together.

13

DRESSAGE LESSON
+ BIO QUIZ
= DISASTER

"PAIGE, I PROMISE I'LL HELP YOU PRACTICE for your audition video tonight," I whispered into my phone. If Mr. Conner saw me in the aisle on the phone, he'd probably throw my cell into the muck pile!

"Okay," Paige said. "Thanks, Sasha."

After hanging up, I put my phone into my coat pocket and unclipped Charm from the crossties. I'd promised to help Paige, but I also had lots of homework in my other classes. I'd been concentrating so hard on biology that I'd let homework in my other classes pile up.

"Ready?" Callie asked as she led Jack beside me. She looked polished in her black and red tartan coat and leather gloves.

It was my first Monday morning practice with Heather

and Callie. As we walked into the arena, I crossed my fingers and hoped we would work on jumping today. If it was dressage, Callie and Heather would *so* kick my butt.

Callie and I led our horses down the aisle and passed the hallway by Mr. Conner's office. I slowed Charm when I heard Julia's voice. Callie stopped Jack beside Charm.

"Well then," Julia said. "Why are you friends with Sasha all of a sudden?"

Callie and I looked at each other.

"Jules, stop it," Heather snapped. "We're not *friends.* Mr. Conner paired us up. We *have* to do lessons together."

"But you let her ride Aristocrat," Julia said.

"I don't have time for this," Heather said. "I have to get to my lesson. Go hang out with your boyfriend or something." Boots tapped down the aisle.

I tugged Charm forward and Callie pulled on Jack's reins. We hurried into the arena.

"Julia's jealous just because Heather and I are forced to ride together?" I asked Callie.

"Obviously," Callie said. "*I* still can't believe that you rode Aristocrat."

Um, hello. Callie didn't have to act so surprised that I could handle another horse.

Heather led Aristocrat into the arena and Mr. Conner stepped in behind her.

"Hello, girls," Mr. Conner said. He smiled as we mounted our horses and lined them up in front of him.

"Hi," we said back.

"Today, we're going to focus on dressage," Mr. Conner announced.

Of course. My favorite.

Callie and Heather high-fived while I put on a fake smile.

Mr. Conner continued. "Dressage is a French term for 'training.' That's exactly what we'll be doing today. During a dressage test, the judges will score mainly based on obedience, suppleness, and accuracy. The lower level dressage course is made up of the letters A-K-E-H-C-M-B-F. Think of it as 'All King Edward's Horses Can Make Big Fences.' You'll either have your test memorized, as preferred, or you'll have someone stand off to the side and call out your test. When you move up to higher levels, you won't be allowed to have an assistant to call for you."

Callie and Heather didn't have anyone read their tests for them.

"The judges will score each move on a scale from

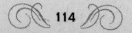

one to ten," Mr. Conner added. "If you complete a difficult move, you'll get more points. A score of seven or eight is respectable." Heather nodded and adjusted her black helmet. She and Callie were our team's best dressage riders.

"If we're not showing in dressage, should we still memorize the course and learn some of the moves?" I asked.

"No," Mr. Conner said. "That's not necessary, but I do want to use this lesson as a supplement to show all of you that obedience in your horses is important. Even if you don't compete in dressage, the lessons will help you in other riding areas."

Maybe dressage would be good for Charm and me.

"Let's get started," Mr. Conner said. "Callie, why don't you perform a couple of moves from your last test and then Heather can ride."

Heather and I backed our horses out of the lettered markers Mr. Conner had set up. Callie urged Black Jack forward at a working trot into the center of the square, or point X. She halted Jack and saluted Mr. Conner. Then Jack continued at a working trot to point M. She made a tight turn and Jack's whole body flowed into the circle. I'd never seen his body move like that. Callie invisibly signaled Jack to do a free walk to marker H. It almost

looked like moves on my Rolex Kentucky DVDs. Jack made another circle and then trotted to the center. Callie halted Jack smoothly and saluted again.

Heather and I clapped and Callie rode Jack out of the arena, barely able to suppress the smile on her face.

"Now, let's talk about Callie's moves and why that was a fantastic test," Mr. Conner said.

"She did her move the second she hit each marker," Heather offered. "She didn't hesitate at all."

I couldn't figure her out. One lesson she knocked Callie and the next she complimented her.

"It looked fluid," I added. "I didn't even see her tell Jack what to do."

Mr. Conner nodded. "Exactly. And that's the point. Did you notice how flexible and relaxed he looked? He almost anticipates her commands. Note that during their free walk, Black Jack just didn't amble along. Callie kept pressure on him with both legs and he worked, even at a relaxed pace, from letter to letter. Let's try something different with Heather, if she's willing."

Heather nodded. She loved any chance to show off.

"I want Sasha and Callie to call out commands and Heather and Aristocrat will perform them," Mr. Conner said. "It's not traditional because Heather hasn't

memorized the moves, but I'm sure she's up for it. Callie, you call first."

Heather halted at X, saluted Mr. Conner, and looked to Callie for her first move.

Callie hesitated for a second then called out, "Working trot to H and then circle." Heather followed Callie's command and Mr. Conner nodded to me.

"Free walk to G and then canter to B," I said. Aristocrat's chestnut legs gleamed as he stretched into a walk to the G marker. The second Heather and Aristocrat reached G, he broke into a collected canter. Heather sat motionless on his back. Aristocrat's stride was almost mesmerizing and Heather looked melded to his back. The girl was good.

"Come back to X at a working trot," Callie called. Heather turned the second Callie gave the command and trotted to the center. Aristocrat stopped and Heather gave her final salute.

"Wow," I breathed to Callie. "That was amazing."

"It was," Callie said, nodding. Our team was going to be awesome at regionals!

"Now, Callie and Heather, you can act as my assistants and help me take Sasha through a couple of beginning exercises. You two may start giving directions." Mr. Conner stepped back to watch us.

I swallowed.

"Want to try the free walk first?" Callie asked.

"Sure." Charm eyed Jack and the two bumped muzzles.

"Okay, you're going to sit deep and push him forward, just a little bit, with your hands and seat. Give him more rein and encourage him to stretch his neck."

It sounded easy, but nothing about dressage was simple. "Can I watch you first?"

"Sure." Callie circled Jack away from Charm and me. She straightened and signaled Jack to walk forward. He lifted his head and started. "I'm giving him tiny cues by squeezing my legs or moving my fingers on the reins. See?"

Jack stepped quickly, but looked as if he placed each hoof down with precision. I nodded.

"All right, Charm," I said. "Let's try it."

I tried to ignore Heather and Mr. Conner, who watched me closely.

I took a breath and sat deep in the saddle, tightening my legs around Charm's sides. He ambled forward and didn't pay much attention. I tried to focus on him, but I kept thinking about the bio quiz I had to take after our lesson. I could *not* get another F.

"Tighten up the reins a bit and urge him forward

while almost holding him back at the same time," Callie offered. She watched through narrowed eyes as she studied Charm's movements.

That sounded like a good way to give Charm mixed signals, but I didn't argue. I did what Callie said. Charm got on the bit and loosened his legs and neck while walking strongly forward. "Ooh!" I said. "Is that it?"

"That looks okay," Callie said. "But you need more leg."

I turned Charm in a circle. Callie was right, but she was embarrassing me in front of Heather!

I let Charm move forward again and applied more pressure with my legs. "Better?"

Callie hesitated. "Yeah, better."

Callie backed off as Heather rode closer. My fingers tightened on the reins as I looked at Heather.

"Let's try something else," Heather said. She looked at Mr. Conner for backup and he nodded. "How about a working trot?"

"Okay," I said.

"For the working trot," Heather said. "You want to get Charm's attention and make sure he's collected. He needs to have an even stride and should be listening to you for the slightest cue."

Heather urged Aristocrat forward. I watched as his trot

became precise and he collected himself under Heather's hands. Every move was near perfect. Heather sat up straight in her navy blue fleece pullover and her bare fingers held the reins firmly. Aristocrat had one ear forward and another back—listening and paying attention to Heather. Heather trotted him to the arena wall and then headed back to me.

"That was nice," Mr. Conner said. "Let's see Sasha and Charm try it."

"Okay," I whispered to Charm. "We can do it." Charm walked forward and he eased into a trot. The reins were taut in my fingers. I half closed my eyes for a second and signaled Charm to follow Black Jack's example and do a working trot. I tried not to look at Heather, but as she watched me, images of her and Jacob talking and laughing popped into my head.

Charm, mouthing the bit, ignored my command to stretch out his legs. "C'mon," I whispered. "You can do this." I had to focus. Otherwise, I was messing things up for both of us.

Charm let out a small huff, arched his neck and started to strike the ground sharper with his hooves. "Good boy." His back rounded and he brought his hindquarters underneath him. We did a working trot that almost, but not

quite, resembled Aristocrat's, then circled and went back to Mr. Conner.

I shook my head. Charm had performed well, but he could tell my mind wasn't on the lesson. I'd made him look bad in front of Aristocrat and Jack.

"Good effort, Sasha," Mr. Conner said. He patted Charm's shoulder and looked up at me. "Charm seems to respond well to these movements."

"He does," I agreed, loosening the reins and letting Charm relax. "This might help me with control during show jumping."

Mr. Conner smiled. "Exactly. And with more focus, I'm sure you'll do even better."

I cringed.

"You girls are free to go. I'll see you at the next lesson," Mr. Conner said.

We nodded and dismounted.

"Good job," Callie said.

But I wondered if she meant it.

"Not really. I didn't focus enough. We could have done better."

"What were you thinking about?"

"My bio quiz," I lied. And then, "Jacob and Heather," I muttered.

Callie pressed her lips together and didn't say a word.

We handed Charm and Jack to Mike and Doug.

"Bye!" I called to Callie as I dashed back to Winchester to shower and change for bio. I'd worry about Callie later. I had to rock this quiz or bad grade + no show = angry teammates. When I got to my room, my text alert chimed.

I think U said U have a bio quiz 2day. Good luck! —Eric

I smiled and tossed the phone on my bed.

Ms. Peterson passed out the biology quizzes. I crossed my fingers on my left hand and wrote my name on the paper with my right. Two rows ahead of me, Julia and Alison scribbled on their papers.

I bent my head and looked at the first question. *What is the purpose of the aorta?* Four choices. A–D. My pencil hovered above answer C—*circulates blood to the body.* I darkened the bubble and moved on to the next question. The classroom wall clock's tick echoed in my head. The smell of formaldehyde from another class's experiment burned my nose.

"You have one minute left," Ms. Peterson said. I glanced at the clock, sure she'd made a mistake. But no.

One minute, one minute, I repeated to myself as I finished checking my work. I furiously erased my answer on

problem five and changed it to A instead of B. The quiz didn't seem insanely hard, but I hadn't thought I'd failed the last one, either.

"And . . . pencils down," Ms. Peterson called. She stepped away from the whiteboard and stood in front of the desks. "Pass your quizzes forward."

I handed my quiz to the guy in front of me. Julia and Alison passed their papers forward and looked back at me for a second. They were counting on me to get a good score so I could go to regionals.

My phone buzzed in my pocket and I quickly flipped it open under the desk. It was from Alison. How did she even get my number?

How'd U do?

? Ok. I think. I texted back.

"All right, class, let's open your books to page ninety-eight and look over today's lesson. You'll get your quizzes back on Friday," Ms. Peterson said.

Throughout class, my eyes kept zeroing in on the pile of quizzes on her desk. Suddenly, from now until Friday's biology class seemed like forever.

I trudged out of my creative writing elective and headed to the library. I had a paper to write for history, prep for

an English quiz to do, and practice problems for algebra to finish.

Inside the library, I found a quiet table in the back and dumped the entire contents of my backpack on the table. I spread my books to one side and got out a sheet of paper. The librarians should have given me my own room; I was here enough!

A couple of hours later, my phone buzzed in my pocket.

My caller ID said *Paige*. "Hi," I whispered. The no-phone rule in the library was strict, but I didn't see any librarians around.

"Where are you?" Paige asked. "You were supposed to help me with my video!"

"Omigod!" I said, forgetting to use my library voice. "I'm so sorry! I was studying and I completely forgot. I'll be right there."

In record time, I was packed and running out of the library.

By the time I got inside the dorm, Paige was proofreading her application essay for the thousandth time.

"I'm so, so sorry," I said. "I had a bad lesson and the bio quiz freaked me out and then—"

"Sash," Paige interrupted. "It's okay! I forgot your bio

quiz was today." She gave me a sheepish smile. "How did it go?"

I tossed my bag on my bed. "Okay. I think. Hopefully."

"Well, if you need to do homework, I can work on this by myself," Paige said. She pushed back the sleeves of her clover green keyhole top. She'd paired it with a black, bubble-hem skirt and she looked application-amazing. "I can do it."

"No way," I said. "If I study for another second, my brain will explode."

Paige smiled.

We packed up our gear and staked out the common room as ours for the evening. I set up the camera while Paige gathered her ingredients and spread them onto the counter.

"What recipe did you pick?" I asked.

"Blackberry crumble," Paige said. She grabbed a bowl of fresh blackberries from the fridge. "I wanted a Southern dish."

"Oooh, that was one of my favorites during the Friday's Great Taste Test."

While I finished setting up the camera, Paige readied her ingredients. She tied an apron around her waist and stepped up to the counter.

"Let's do it!" Paige said.

I peered at the camera's digital screen. I pushed the on button and the camera's red light started blinking.

"Paige Parker's winning audition for The Food Network for Kids. Take one. Ready and . . . action!"

Paige smiled and started the dialogue she'd rehearsed. "Hi, everyone! I'm Paige Parker—welcome to my kitchen! Today, we've got a sweet treat guaranteed to give you a taste of summer during the winter months. We're baking a Southern dessert favorite—blackberry crumble."

I kept my eyes on the screen. Paige sounded like a pro! She wasn't even nervous in front of the camera.

"First, let's preheat the oven to 350 degrees," Paige said. She turned on the oven, while keeping her back from the camera. "Next, let's run through our ingredients. We've got two and a half cups of blackberries, a two-thirds cup of sugar, the juice from one lemon, three tablespoons of butter, a two-thirds cup of flour, and a pinch of salt."

Paige pulled out a glass baking dish. "Now, pour the blackberries into this pan and sprinkle half of your sugar over them." Paige did and I watched her movements through the camera. "Add the lemon juice and then get a clean bowl."

Under the counter, Paige pulled out a bowl and carefully added the rest of the ingredients. She creamed them and then sprinkled it over the berries.

"We'll pop this into the oven at 350 degrees for forty minutes," Paige said as she slipped the pan into the oven. "When the crumble's top is golden-brown, it's done! I've got one already made, so let's see . . ."

Paige put on yellow oven mitts and reached into the second oven. She pulled out a dish that smelled heavenly. "Ooh, it looks good!" she said. She cut out a small square and put it on a plate. Paige held it up to the camera. "There you go! Blackberry crumble to satisfy your sweet tooth any day."

She totally deserved her own network!

"Thanks for joining me. I hope to see you again soon!" Paige grabbed a fork and took a delicate bite of crumble. "Bye!"

"And . . . we're done!" I said when I pushed the off button. "You're amazing, Paige! You sounded so professional. I don't even think we need a second take."

Paige squeezed her hands together. "Really? Yay! Want some?"

"Do you have to ask?" I took the plate and let the warm blackberries melt over my tongue.

"I'll help you clean up," I said after we'd eaten our desserts. "You're so going to get this."

Paige turned to me with an armful of dirty dishes. "I hope so. I'll format the DVD and give it to Livvie to mail tomorrow. Then, all we can do is wait!"

Yeah, for my quiz grade, for the Sweetheart Soirée, for regionals, and now for Paige's news. Waiting never got any easier.

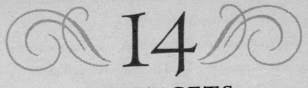

14

SASHA GETS
A BROTHER

REGIONALS WERE EIGHT DAYS AWAY, BUT judging by the expression on Ms. Peterson's face, my chances of going didn't look good.

"These were not the best batch of quizzes," Ms. Peterson said. She frowned at us from her spot at the front of the classroom. She adjusted the glasses perched on her head and held the papers close to her chest so no one could see the grades. "From most of you, I expect more studying. But for a lucky few, your grades reflect your hard work."

Well, it was over. No way was my grade in the latter category. In my biology class experience, hard work didn't always translate to good grades. I hunched down into my seat to avoid Ms. Peterson's gaze as she passed our quizzes back. She moved around the room and put the papers facedown on the desks.

The guy next to me turned his over, pumped a fist in the air and then high-fived the girl next to him.

Please let it at least be a B–, I repeated in my head. *Or even a C+.*

Ms. Peterson paused by my desk and put down my quiz. I looked at her and she gave me a slight nod.

With one eye shut, I lifted up the corner of the paper and looked. B+. Oh, my God! A B+?! I grabbed the paper in my hands and looked again to be sure I wasn't hallucinating.

Julia and Alison turned to look at me.

"What'd you get?" Alison mouthed.

"B plus," I mouthed back.

Alison nodded and Julia sighed before whispering, "Good."

The riding team needed this.

Under my desk, I pulled out my phone and texted Paige. *B+!!* I wrote and sent the message.

Seconds later, *U rock, SS! *</ :^)* appeared on my screen. And for just a minute, I'd agree with her.

I wasn't even out of the classroom when I dialed Union's library and asked for Mom. "Sasha?" Mom answered. "Are you okay?"

I never called her at work unless it was an emergency. The last time I'd called her there, I'd set an Arby's sandwich on fire in the microwave when I'd tried to reheat it in the foil. I stopped by the water fountain. "I got my quiz back," I said.

"And?"

"B plus!"

"Sasha! Way to go, honey. I'm so proud of you."

"Thanks, Mom," I said. Out of the corner of my eye, I saw Mr. Lane, my creative writing teacher, giving me the *get off the phone now* look. "Gotta go. Love you," I said and shut my phone before she could answer.

I walked down the hallway with a giant grin on my face. I couldn't wait to see Charm after school and tell him. I didn't even care that we had a pairs lesson with Heather today. But along my way, a flash of red caught my eye on the bulletin board.

It was a red flyer shaped like a connected XO. I squinted to read the fancy script.

The Sweetheart Soirée is drawing near.
Do you have your eye on someone dear?
Even if so, you must come solo.
Bringing a date is a definite no-no.

No dates? That seemed odd for Valentine's Day . . . which I now realized was three weeks away! Well, at least I wouldn't have to worry about asking Jacob.

I tore myself away from the flyer and slipped into class. After this period, I'd have to take a pic of the flyer for Paige in case she didn't see it yet. We could play Nancy Drew and look for any secret messages together.

Charm and Aristocrat huffed as Heather and I slowed them. We'd spent most of our lesson on flat work, coaching each other's seats. And we hadn't even argued once.

"Ready to cool them out?" Heather asked.

"Yeah, Charm's pretty warm," I said.

Charm and I were ambling around the arena when my phone buzzed. I slid it out of my coat pocket.

"Hey, *Jacob*," I said, emphasizing his name so Heather would hear me. "What's up?"

I watched Heather's head snap around and her mouth tighten.

"Hey, Sash," Jacob said. "You busy?"

"Nope, just finished my riding lesson."

"Still doing that horse thing, huh?" Jacob teased.

"Yeah, but I might trade him in for a car in a few years," I joked back. Charm's ears swiveled back toward me. I covered the phone with my hand. "Just kidding, boy," I whispered to Charm. He snorted in relief.

"I've got to write a paper about life in the South for my English class. We're supposed to read a classic book about it and I can't think of a good one. Got any recommendations?"

"I'm reading *Huck Finn*," I said. "That's a good one. Or try *Tom Sawyer*. Have you read those?"

Heather reined Aristocrat closer and practically tipped off his side as she listened.

"Nope. I did see the old Disney movie of *Tom Sawyer*," Jacob said with a laugh. "I think I'll try that book."

"If you need help, IM me or something," I said.

After we hung up, I put the phone back in my pocket and Charm and I continued to circle the arena.

"You're such a good sister," Heather said.

"Sister?" I asked.

"That's so sweet of you to help your brother with English class."

"That wasn't my brother," I told her.

Heather rolled her eyes. "Sure it was. You had him call and pretend to be Jacob. How creative."

I pulled Charm to a halt and glared at her. "It *wasn't* my brother! I'm an only child!"

Heather circled Aristocrat sharply and headed out of the arena. "Sure, whatever you say," she said through raspberry-tinted lips. "Later."

"We're NOT getting another shirtless Nick Ryan film," I told Paige. "We've watched him for the last three weekends. I need a new visual!" I put my phone on my other ear as I walked to the media center. I'd volunteered to go out and rent a video for our usual Friday night flick.

Paige laughed and I heard popcorn popping in the background. "Fine. You pick the guy this time."

"Will do." I put my phone away and stepped into the crowded media center. People were lined up for snacks and movie tickets.

I stuck my hands in the pocket of my UConn hoodie and passed one of the common rooms.

Wait, *what*? I backed up and peered through the glass window on the door.

Jacob.

Callie.

The Trio. And a few other people packed the closed-door common room. MTV was on the plasma television and sodas, chips, and candy filled the table. Heather sat next to Jacob on the blue couch. Callie was laughing and

talking to one of the guys on the eighth-grade riding team. Julia and Alison were listening to a story that Ben was telling them.

I couldn't believe it—this couldn't be a coincidence. Someone had planned it. The same someone had also conveniently left my name off the invite list. I'm guessing it was the blonde in the sparkly pink shirt and low-rise jeans sitting next to MY film partner.

Calm down, I told myself. *Don't go all crazy jealous girl on him. Guys HATE that.* But that wasn't all I was worried about—besides Jacob, what was Callie doing hanging with the Trio? We each had separate friends, but I didn't know she partied with them. Or with Jacob.

When I pushed the door open, Heather was the first one to look at me. Jacob's head was craned in the opposite direction as he talked to one of the other guys. Heather flashed her teeth at me in a giant grin and scooted closer to Jacob.

"Hi," I said over the roar of the TV. Callie's head snapped around and she jumped up for the remote.

"You're so late," she said. She turned down the volume.

"Late?" I questioned. "I wasn't invited."

"What?" Callie asked.

The three girls and one guy I didn't know glanced at me before busying themselves with a bowl of chips.

"No one told me to come," I said, eyeing Jacob and Heather on the couch.

Jacob hopped up and walked over to me. "Didn't Heather ask you to come?" he asked.

I shook my head.

"Sorry," Heather yawned. "Guess I forgot. But you're here now, right?"

Please. No one was buying that. She pulled this Witch with a capital W move on purpose.

"She said she asked you," Callie whispered. "Heather told me you had a dorm meeting with Livvie. Sash, I swear. I'm sorry."

"C'mon," Jacob said. He plopped back on the couch and waved at me. "Stay."

I ignored him and started to turn toward the door.

Heather stood up and walked over to me. She got inches away from my face so Jacob couldn't hear. "Better get used to it, Sasha." She turned back to Jacob and put on her angel face. "Stay, Sasha," she said in a loud voice. "We were just about to watch a movie."

"I've got to go," I said. My stomach churned, and I could feel an angry sting of tears threatening to spill

over my eyes. "My roommate's waiting for me."

"I'm going with you," Callie said. She grabbed her black coat off the recliner.

"You don't have to," I said.

"I want to." Callie's voice was firm. I didn't even look at Jacob on my way out—and I noticed that he didn't exactly try to stop me, either. If Jacob wanted to stay, fine. I didn't want to talk to him now anyway.

Callie followed me to the movie rental room. She shuffled quietly behind me without saying a word.

"Paige and I are watching a movie, if you want to come," I offered. My eyes scanned the racks of films.

Callie gave me a grateful smile. "Definitely. And you should know . . . Jacob didn't do anything wrong—I was there the whole time. Heather didn't even sit by him until two seconds before you came in."

I blew out a breath. "Thanks for telling me," I said. But he was still hanging out with her now. They were in there watching a movie together, so it was obvious that he'd rather be spending time with her than me.

When my text alert sounded, I looked down, half expecting it to be Jacob, apologizing for what had happened. Maybe he'd want to talk in person. But when I read the name on my screen, my heart sunk. It was only Eric.

Hey, Sash! Hope 2 C U 2mrw @ the stable.

I sighed.

"Not him, huh?" Callie asked.

"Nope—just Eric," I said. "So, what kind of movie are you in the mood for?"

"Can we forget the movie for a sec?" Callie asked. "You know Eric likes you, right? *Like*-likes you."

I rolled my eyes. "No he doesn't."

"He does too. He texts you, he's always smiling at you—and he runs over to talk to you every time you're around him."

I almost laughed. "Please. He's new—he just wants someone to talk to. He doesn't like me that way."

Callie shrugged. "Whatever you say."

We browsed the rest of the shelves, but I couldn't pay attention. I let Callie pick the movies and pretended to care when she asked me if the choices were okay.

I knew Callie was wrong about Eric liking me, so it didn't even bother me if she didn't believe me. What bothered me wasn't what Callie said, it was what she hadn't said—she hadn't said that *Jacob like*-liked me.

15

GROUNDED

"C'MON, GUYS," MR. CONNER SAID. "WHAT DO you think this is, Monday morning?"

The Trio, Callie, and I had been yawning all morning. It was barely seven thirty on Monday morning and Mr. Conner had gathered us for a group lesson. The show was less than two weeks away—and we had some serious practicing to do. Gray light filtered through the arena windows and Mr. Conner flipped on the overhead fluorescent lights.

"Start warming them up and then we'll do drills," Mr. Conner said.

Callie and I followed the Trio and began circling in the arena. Up ahead, Julia and Alison had pulled Trix and Sunstruck side by side so they could whisper.

"Wonder what they're talking about," I whispered to Callie.

Callie looked over to be sure Mr. Conner wasn't watching. Talking in class was the number one way to get kicked out of a lesson. "What else? The Sweetheart Soirée. It's ALL they talk about."

"Are you going?" I asked.

"Definitely," Callie said. "It's supposed to be amazing."

"Do you know what time it starts?" I asked. "I haven't seen any flyers that say that."

"One of the Orchard girls said she heard it starts at eight," Callie said. "She said that the start time is always word-of-mouth."

"Girls!" Mr. Conner called out. "Now that you've warmed up your mouths, let's get the rest of you warmed up. Please stand in your stirrups and trot."

Callie and I whisper-groaned to each other. That was one of the *worst* torture exercises ever!

The five of us stood in the stirrups and hovered over our horses' necks. I braced my hands against Charm's neck so I wouldn't jerk on his mouth if I wobbled.

We made three circles around the arena before Mr. Conner nodded to us to sit.

"Move them into a slow canter and then change gaits

as I call them," he said. "Try to switch gaits in as few strides as possible."

The horses increased their speed to a rocking canter and Sunstruck's palomino tail fanned out in front of me. Alison rocked with the Arabian's smooth gait and for a second, I imagined Sunstruck galloping across the desert. He looked like the Black Stallion's lighter cousin.

"Trot," Mr. Conner called.

I applied pressure to Charm's mouth and he slowed after three strides. He tossed his head in annoyance—he loved cantering and wanted to keep doing it. I rubbed his neck with one hand to soothe him.

As we went around the arena, my gaze and my focus settled on Heather. I tried not to get angry, but seeing her now made me think about Friday night all over again. Jacob had never even texted or called that night—and I hadn't spoken to Heather since I'd stormed out of her little party.

"Canter," Mr. Conner called.

Charm must have understood Mr. Conner's command because he cantered before I tapped him with my leg. At least *he* was listening. Ahead of us, Sunstruck continued to trot rather than canter and Charm almost ran up his heels! I veered Charm to the right and kept him from colliding with Sunstruck.

"Alison!" I shouted. "Canter!"

"Oh! Sorry!" Alison snapped out of her apparent day-dream and Sunstruck started to canter.

"Walk and bring them to the center, please," Mr. Conner said. His tone was stern. He frowned at us and we lined up in front of him. "What's going on?"

Silence. The horses chomped on the bit and Trix started to crabstep.

"Anyone?" Mr. Conner questioned. "Can someone please tell me what is distracting you so much this morning that is more important than practicing for regionals?"

We looked at each other guiltily. Charm lowered his head, too. Mr. Conner walked back and forth in front of us, his black boots scuffing in the arena dirt.

"Dismount," Mr. Conner said. "Maybe you'll pay more attention from the ground."

I dismounted and stood beside Charm. Thoughts of the Sweetheart Soirée and Heather and Jacob flew out of my head. Charm and I had to concentrate or I'd be assigned mucking duty.

When Mr. Conner finally let us go, we were sweaty, dusty, and exhausted. He'd made us lead the horses for half of the lesson—by the time I'd mounted Charm, my legs had been sore and I'd barely been able to catch my breath.

"We're gonna be late for class!" Callie yelped, looking at her watch.

Together, we hurried out of the arena and pulled our horses behind us.

Heather led Aristocrat past me and handed him to Mike. "I can't be late. I mean, I was hoping to run into, oh, I don't know, *Jacob* in the hallway."

My fingers tightened on the reins.

"We're supposed to meet up later but—"

"What's your problem?" I snapped. "Do you like him?"

Heather laughed and put her hands in the pockets of her tweed coat. "Does it matter if *I* like him? He likes me—isn't that what's most important?"

Doug stepped up to me and reached for Charm's reins. "Sash, let go, please," he whispered.

"Oh." I looked down at my hands and saw my knuckles were white. "Sorry." I released the reins and Doug led Charm away.

"C'mon," Callie said. She tugged my hand. "We've got to go. We're already late."

Without another look at Heather, we headed down the aisle.

"I have to stop thinking about Jacob and Heather!" I said. "It's messing with my riding."

Callie nodded. "Obsess all you want *after* regionals. But you've got to focus. You don't want to blow it because of them."

"I know. You're right."

I didn't know how Callie did it—she was always so focused. And even though she was my BFF, I knew it wouldn't feel too good if Callie swept all of her classes at regionals and I didn't even place in *one*.

We walked up the sidewalk and I sucked in a breath of cold air. The late January temps were still freezing and we'd had sleet and a light snow last night. Frozen grass poked through the thin layer of snow. I half-wished for a blizzard so I wouldn't have to see Heather for a day.

At the other end of campus, a guy in a dark red winter hat and a black coat waved at me. When I squinted my eyes, I saw that it was Eric. Even across campus, I could see his smile.

Callie and I waved back.

"Don't even say it," I warned Callie in a grumpy voice.

Callie pretend-zipped her lips shut, but I could tell she was suppressing a big-time *told you so*.

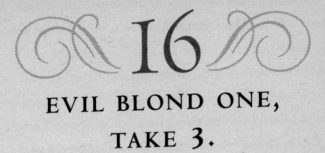

16

EVIL BLOND ONE,
TAKE 3.

BY WEDNESDAY, PAIGE AND I HAD BECOME pros at the art of distraction.

Paige had baked so many apple crisps that instead of getting better, they got worse.

I'd spent too much time staring into space and reorganizing my iPod when I should have been studying.

"Why don't you just call him?" Paige asked, looking up from the math homework on her desk.

"This roommate thing is a little weird—you can read my mind now?"

"It doesn't take a mind reader," Paige said gently.

"I do want to see him," I admitted. "He's usually playing games at the media center now. Maybe I should walk over there."

Paige put down her green pen. "Okay. But call him if you don't find him. Just tell him how you feel. Get some answers."

"I promise," I said. "Wish me luck."

On my walk across campus, I called Mom. I'd been too busy with school and riding to talk to my parents much.

"Hi, honey!" she answered. "How's your week going?"

"Fine," I said. Even though it was babyish, talking to Mom or Dad always made me feel better. "I'm looking for my friend Jacob." Oops! Probably shouldn't have said that. Mom and Dad knew I'd been IMing with a guy during break, but they didn't know who.

"Well," Mom said slowly. "I hope you find him. I think. Dad and I are getting ready for your show. We're excited!"

"Me, too! Charm's ready."

"You're *both* ready."

"I guess," I said. "How's Dad doing?"

"Oh, good. He . . ."

As my mother launched into a story about my dad's fantasy football league, I neared the string of little shops by the media center. I passed the Sweet Shoppe—the cozy store on campus that sold the best coffee, muffins, and hot chocolate. I shivered—maybe a cup of something warm to go wasn't such a bad idea.

But as soon as I walked inside, my eyes stopped on a table near the fireplace. My mouth dropped open. Heather, sipping from a ceramic coffee mug, sat directly across from Jacob. They had a pile of books between them and . . . they looked sickeningly adorable together.

"Mom," I said into the phone, trying not to sound as devastated as I felt. "I gotta go. Call you later."

Heather and Jacob were so deep in conversation, they didn't even notice me. Jacob's head tilted toward Heather. He had on his favorite hoodie—the one with Homer Simpson that said "Slacker." The one he told me he was only allowed to wear outside of class. Heather wore a deep purple sweater that was pretty on her and made her blond hair look even blonder and more perfect-looking.

I felt my chest get warm. How had I been so blind? Heather and Jacob, in the library. Heather and Jacob, in the rec room on the couch together. Heather and Jacob at the Sweet Shoppe. I wasn't Jacob's girlfriend and I never would be—*Heather* was Jacob's girlfriend—I was his film class partner. *Assigned* film class partner.

I stepped backward out the door and onto the crunchy, frozen-over grass, unable to pull my eyes away from the couple inside. Finally, I forced myself to turn around and walk away.

I didn't know where I was going, but I couldn't go back to the dorm. Paige would ask me questions about Jacob or try to make me feel better. I didn't want to talk about Jacob right now.

A new wave of tears threatened to spill out of my eyes. I suddenly felt furious. If Jacob liked Heather, he should have told me! I'd probably completely embarrassed myself accusing Heather of stealing Jacob from me . . . when the truth was, he was never mine to be stolen.

When I snapped back to reality, I found myself in front of the library. I had been planning to come later today to get the books I needed for my English paper.

"Just do it now," I grumbled to myself. At least it would give me something to do, other than mope over Jacob. But before I went inside, pulled out my phone. After this, I would be done—but I needed someone sane to talk me down a little before I went inside.

I plopped onto the icy step, not caring that my butt would freeze, and pressed speed dial 2.

"What's up?" Callie asked.

"I saw Heather and Jacob together in the Sweet Shoppe," I blurted out.

"Uh-oh. Were they kissing?" she asked.

"No."

"Hugging?"

"Um, *no*."

"Then what?" Callie asked, her tone bordering impatient. "Making googly eyes at each other over chai lattes?"

"They were *sitting* together," I said.

"Sitting together," Callie repeated. "And you're mad because . . ."

What part of "The Evil Blond One is Stealing My Guy" didn't she understand?

"But they're hanging out together! Again! And Heather is really pretty and has a perfect wardrobe and is an amazing rider and Jacob probably really, really likes her! I see them together all the time, Cal. I think they're going out."

"Sash," Callie said. "If Jacob liked Heather, he'd tell you. He's a good guy. You guys were texting all the time over break, and before that, he came to the winter dance for you. And he danced with you—a *lot*. You said they were just sitting together. And if you overreact, it'll freak him out. Chill."

I stared at the icy ground, suddenly feeling the frigid temperature. "I don't know," I said. "I mean, maybe you're right. Ugh! Why is this so hard?"

Callie was quiet for a second. "Just don't worry about it. If you see them kissing, then we'll make her sorry. Until then, either ask Jacob what's going on or let it go. You're making yourself crazy."

"Okay, okay." I took a deep breath. "You're right." I stood up. "Thank you for being such a good friend. I'll text you later?"

"Definitely," Callie said.

We hung up and I stepped inside the library. Maybe researching dead poets would distract me. Nothing in the present was working.

17

S & S

I'D JUST WALKED OUT OF MY LAST CLASS ON Monday when my phone rang. I blinked at the phone screen again. Jacob!

"Hi," I said.

"Hey, Sash! I haven't seen you around much in the last week."

"Oh, yeah, I've been really busy," I said. And kind of avoiding you.

"Got any free time soon?"

"Um, sure."

"I finished the editing on our film and I wanted you to see it. Can you meet me at the media center in about an hour?"

Oh. It was school-related. He *had* to see me.

"See you then." I hung up and trudged back to Winchester to unload my books.

Jacob found me sitting on the couch in one of the smaller common rooms at the media center.

"Hey," he said, smiling. He tugged off his black coat and tossed it on the table.

"Hi." Even though I didn't want to smile, I did. He always looked unbelievably cute—it didn't matter what he wore. We both wore jeans and black sweaters—but mine was accessorized with my letter S necklace and my silver charm bracelet.

"Wait till you see," Jacob said. "It's got music and credits and everything. It looks just like a real documentary."

"Really?" Excitement crept into my voice. But I was still mad at him. "How'd you do the music?"

Jacob popped the DVD into the player and sat next to me on the couch. "Made it. My friend Trent has a band. He composed it himself."

"Wow. That was such a great idea." Our eyes locked for a second.

Jacob hit play and scooted closer to me. His arm brushed against mine.

I tried to take even breaths. *Relax,* I told myself. *Just see what happens.* But he couldn't be here with me, brushing his arm against mine, if he was going out with Heather. It had to have been an accident.

Right?

The TV lit up. A piano score streamed through the speakers and indigo-blue words began to scroll across the screen. *S & S presents an original major motion picture. Starring Sasha Silver, Jacob Schwartz, and Charm. Directed by Jacob Schwartz.*

"This is so cool!" I said. Without thinking, I reached over and took Jacob's hand. He didn't even hesitate to grab mine back. I could feel my face flushing bright red.

As we watched the short film, I realized Jacob wasn't letting go of my hand.

The credits rolled all too soon. I could have sat like this for another hour. Or two.

For a minute, neither of us moved. I started to feel self-conscious of my own heartbeat. Could he hear it as well as I could? Jacob turned to me, his warm hand still folded over mine.

"We're movie stars now," I blurted out, wanting to fill the silence.

"Well," Jacob said. "You're more of a star than me."

"Oh," I said, blushing again. "Well, you did a really good job editing it."

Jacob let go of my hand to eject the DVD and turned back to look at me. "I've kind of . . ." His eyes flickered down and then back at me. ". . . um, missed you lately."

!!!!!

"Me too," I said.

"Sorry things were weird that night with Heather," he said. "She must have gotten confused about who she invited. I left five minutes after you."

"But I thought—"

Jacob shook his head. "I only went because I thought you'd be there."

I looked down at my hands in my lap, hoping he'd reach out to hold my hand again. I wanted to believe him, but I was still thinking about seeing him with Heather at the Sweet Shoppe.

"So," Jacob said. "Are we . . . okay?"

I smiled when he picked up one of my hands again.

"Because I was wondering if you're going to the Sweetheart Soirée?"

I tried not to look as if I'd been waiting weeks for him

to ask me about it. "Yes," I barely choked out. "With, um, Paige and Callie."

"Right. Because you can't show up with a date, right?"

Eeeeee! Just hearing the word "date" was enough to wake the butterflies in my stomach.

"Right," I said. "No dates—at least, that's what the flyer said."

Jacob squeezed my hand. "Well, I'll just have to look for you there, then."

I fought the urge to re-gloss.

"I guess that would be okay." I smiled.

"Oh, you guess?" Jacob laughed. "Well, do you guess it might be okay if I treat you to a hot chocolate?"

"Yeah," I sighed. "I guess that you could lure me with hot chocolate. As long as it has marshmallows."

Jacob laughed and pulled me to my feet. "You're very demanding."

At the Sweet Shoppe, we sat across from each other in a booth. It was warm inside and I was giddy with excitement. It felt like our first few get-togethers last fall.

"Mmm," I said, licking hot chocolate off my lips. "So good!"

Jacob stuck his spoon in his mug and fished around for

marshmallows. When he found some, he spooned them into my mug.

Swoon.

"So," he said, "What's going on with riding?"

"I've got regionals on Saturday," I said. "I've been practicing like crazy."

"Regionals? That's a big deal, right?"

I swallowed my sip of marshmallows, nodding. "I'm trying not to get nervous."

"Don't be." Jacob smiled. "You'll do great."

"I hope so."

"Here's to first place," Jacob said, raising his mug.

"And to movie stardom," I said, holding mine up.

We laughed and clinked our glasses together.

"So I guess Jacob isn't going out with Heather!" I squealed into my phone. I was walking back to Winchester and had called Callie the second Jacob had left. I quickly highlighted all of the good parts from the past hour.

"Told you!" Callie said. "They're just friends."

"He wants to see me at the Soirée," I said, pulling my scarf up over my chin.

"We'll make sure you look gorgeous," Callie assured me. "I've got to study right now. But call me later?"

"Later," I agreed.

I enjoyed the slow, quiet walk across campus back to my dorm. A few snowflakes floated from the sky. I stopped, turned my face upward and took a minute to breathe. Things finally felt good again.

18

TOMORROW, TOMORROW!

TGIF WAS AN UNDERSTATEMENT. THIS WEEK, I'd aced an English quiz and Paige had finished her history project.

I was exhausted from another grueling week of practice, but Mr. Conner wasn't letting up. The show was tomorrow and he wanted us prepared. I was definitely prepared—prepared to drop. The grimaces on the Trio's and Callie's faces at practice suggested they wanted a day off, too.

"Tighten up the reins, Sasha! Alison, more inside leg!" Mr. Conner's voice reverberated off the indoor arena walls and caused Charm to shake his head. He'd been making us do drills—walk, trot, canter—for the past two hours and my legs felt like they were about to fall off.

Charm, Aristocrat, Sunstruck, Trix, and Black Jack sweated from effort, but Mr. Conner hadn't eased up for a second. Callie caught my eye and grimaced. A few strides in front of me, Heather cringed when Mr. Conner focused on her. I almost felt sorry for her. Almost.

"Heather, deepen your seat," Mr. Conner said. "You're not a jockey and this isn't the Derby."

Heather nodded. I watched her back go ramrod straight as she settled into Aristocrat's saddle.

This had been the toughest practice yet. A long, hot shower was the first thing I'd do when I got back to Winchester. I needed a good night's sleep before the show.

"Okay, pull them up." Mr. Conner moved to the arena's center. With a grateful sigh, I halted Charm. We turned the horses to face Mr. Conner and Alison slid Sunstruck into an empty spot next to Charm and me. "Let's talk about how tomorrow is going to go."

"It's going to be a long day," Alison whispered to me. Dirt smudged her right cheek. I was glad I couldn't see my reflection—I knew I looked like a mess.

"*So* long," I replied.

"You'll arrive here by four in the morning," Mr. Conner said. "I don't want the trip to be stressful for the

horses. You'll need to have them wrapped and blanketed early. The Canterwood van will leave at five sharp. If you or your horses are late, you will not be coming. We're on a tight schedule—we've got to make this trip as easy for the horses as possible." He looked at our solemn faces and winked. "And maybe we'll try to make it fun for you, too."

I knew I wasn't the only one relieved—everyone relaxed visibly. For the past week, Mr. Conner had been making regionals sound about as fun as a field trip to the city sewer. Charm shifted under my weight. He craned his neck to look over at Black Jack, who stood next to Trix.

"All right," Mr. Conner said. "Now that you've had a break, let's run through a couple of jumps. Alison, you're up first. You're going to take the oxer, the faux brush, and then the in-and-out. Okay?"

Alison nodded. She spun Sunstruck in a small circle and trotted him away from the jumps before urging him into a canter. Her ponytail flopped against her back as Sunstruck's stride lengthened into a quick canter. He pro-pelled forward over the red-and-white oxer. Alison checked him and then sat quietly as he thundered over the green brush and churned up dirt as he popped over the tight in-and-out.

Mr. Conner smiled and nodded. "Good. Go ahead, Callie."

Callie and Black Jack took the jumps without a problem. Julia and Heather followed and both received nods from Mr. Conner—his methods were tough, but I knew today's workout had really prepped us for tomorrow's jumps.

"Sasha and Charm," Mr. Conner said finally.

Charm must have recognized his name because he yanked on the reins and I almost lost my grip.

"Easy, shh." I stroked his neck with one hand and tapped my heels against his sides. He sidestepped across the arena. He was high-strung today, even for a Thoroughbred! "We're going—cool it," I murmured in his ear.

We circled twice before I let him straighten and pointed him at the oxer. *Three, two, one, squeeze!* My tired legs gripped Charm's sides and he launched into the air, landing easily on the other side. We swept past Callie and the Trio—but my focus didn't break for a second. When you're guiding a thousand-pound horse over jumps, distraction isn't an option. Soon, we were a stride in front of the brush. Charm tucked his front legs and lifted into the air. The brush waved in the breeze from his body.

"Great job. Keep going."

I let him out a notch and we popped over the in-and-out. I patted his neck vigorously and slowed him. We rode up by Black Jack and the two horses sniffed muzzles and huffed a happy greeting to each other.

"That was an excellent practice," Mr. Conner said. He finally took his hands off his hips. "You've all worked incredibly hard to prepare for this show. But I want you all to know that we don't practice this intensely just for shows. We're working hard to make sure you're ready for whatever riding opportunities come your way. Be sure you're packed and get some rest tonight."

We nodded back.

"Now, the farrier and vet are here to check out the competing horses. After they're cool and groomed, please stay while your horse is checked for tomorrow."

"Ouch," Callie said as she and Jack joined Charm and me.

"No kidding," I told her, rubbing the sides of my legs.

We dismounted and walked our horses up and down the aisle for a few minutes. When they were cool, we split up to crosstie them. Charm shook out his coat when I took off the saddle and pad. I put the saddle upside down

on the counter—it was due for a scrub. Charm's gold nameplate on the cantle was dingy.

Charm stood with a back hoof cocked in relaxation as I slipped a cotton lead rope over his neck. I pulled the bridle off his head, careful not to clank the bit against his teeth. He stood still for the halter. I groomed him while we waited for the farrier and vet.

"Hello, Sasha and Charm," Dr. Staton, Canterwood's vet, said as she entered the aisle and walked up to me. I'd met Dr. Staton in the fall, but this was her first time examining Charm since he'd been checked the summer before we'd come to Canterwood.

Dr. Staton's dark blond hair was pulled back into a low ponytail and she wore jeans and a polo shirt. She carried a medical bag and wore a stethoscope around her neck.

"Hi, beautiful boy," she said. She extended her hand to Charm and let him sniff her before she moved to rub his shoulder. I hadn't told Charm she was coming—he was scared of needles. And medical professionals. But Dr. Staton seemed friendly.

"Let's take a listen to his heart and lungs, okay?"

"Okay." I went to Charm's head to keep him calm. I could watch Dr. Staton from here. Learning horse care

was essential since I wanted to run my own breeding and training farm some day.

Dr. Staton took off the stethoscope and put the ends in her ears. She moved the metal disc around Charm's barrel and then placed it behind his elbow. She checked her watch and nodded. "Great pulse and his breathing is perfect. How often do you ride him?"

"Almost every day," I said. "He gets lots of exercise."

Dr. Staton smiled. "I can tell. Want to listen?"

"I'd love to!" I'd never listened to Charm's heart before. I moved over beside her and she handed me the stethoscope. I put in the earpieces and Dr. Staton pointed to where I should move my hand. Charm's heartbeat flooded my ears. It was slower than mine; Each beat pulsed through the stethoscope. I held my breath. That was my horse's heartbeat. It was amazing. I listened for a few seconds before handing the instrument back to Dr. Staton.

"Thank you so much," I said. "I've never heard anything like that!"

"You never get tired of hearing it," she said.

She checked Charm's teeth, eyes, and ears.

"Is he in good shape to compete?" I asked.

"He certainly is," Dr. Staton said. "Let's worm him and then he's good to go."

Charm *hated* being wormed. I moved to hold his head while Dr. Staton readied the worming tube. She stuck the tube in the right corner of Charm's mouth and squeezed. "Easy," I murmured to Charm. He jerked his head up and tried to evade the disgusting yellow paste. The crossties strained against his halter and I tightened my grip on the lead line.

"Almost there, big guy," Dr. Staton said. She expelled the final bit of paste. Charm swallowed several times and tried to rid his mouth of the awful taste.

"It's okay, boy," I soothed. "It's over."

Dr. Staton tossed the dewormer tube in the trash can. "All right, he's ready to go. Good luck at the show. I'll see him this fall."

"Great, thank you." I smiled at her as she moved off to check the rest of the horses. "Okay, Charm," I told him. "Now, we'll get you new shoes. What do you think? Chucks or Skechers?"

The farrier, Mr. O'Brady, walked over to us with his case of tools.

"Hi, Sasha," he said. He patted Charm's shoulder and smiled. "Has it really been six weeks since I've seen him?"

I nodded. "Be sure to give him special show shoes."

165

Mr. O'Brady nodded his bald head. "Show shoes, huh? I'll see what I can do." I stood by Charm's head and watched as Mr. O'Brady removed Charm's old shoes, picked his hooves and used a sharp hoof knife to smooth the hoof. Then, he trimmed off a bit of the hoof and used a rasp to file it down. Charm blinked calmly at me—he never stressed about getting his hooves done. "Good boy," I said when Mr. O'Brady used a hammer to pound the nails into Charm's hoof. Charm flicked his ears but didn't flinch at the sound of the hammer.

A few stalls down, Eric stepped out into the aisle and waved when he saw me.

"Hey," he said, walking over. Bits of hay clung to his black breeches. His boots looked as if Luna had slobbered on them after she had taken a drink of water.

"Hi, Eric." I smiled.

"Just wanted to wish you luck tomorrow," he said. "Not that you need it."

"We definitely need it," I said.

Mr. O'Brady started the last shoe.

Eric gave Charm a final pat on the shoulder and headed out.

"Gotta go—but I'll catch you later," he said.

I waved good-bye to him.

"See," said a voice in my ear.

I jumped and turned to see Callie raising her eyebrows at me.

"He so likes you," she said.

"Stop it!" I hissed.

"So now," Callie said. "You've got *two* guys who like you. You know, I . . . I kind of wish Eric liked me."

My mouth fell open in one of those clichéd movie moments.

"Really?" I asked.

Callie nodded. "He's a rider, he's cute, and he doesn't call me 'dude' like half of the guys in class."

I wasn't sure what to say. Callie had never admitted to liking any guys at school. She was all about riding and studying. But apparently, Eric was the exception.

"You should talk to him," I said. "He would like you."

Callie smiled. "Maybe. But first—regionals."

"Right," I said. "Regionals." I was glad the conversation had switched back to something that was more familiar territory for both me and Callie.

With a wave, Callie headed back to Jack.

After Mr. O'Brady had checked the last shoe, I led Charm to his stall.

"See you tomorrow, boy," I whispered. "Get a good night's sleep!"

On my way back to Winchester, I found Jacob sitting on a stone bench and reading *Tom Sawyer*. The collar on his black coat was pulled up to his chin and he tapped a foot against the cobblestones while he read.

"That must be good if you're reading out in the cold," I said.

Jacob looked up at me and smiled. "It's definitely good. And my roommate messed up a chem experiment in our room, so it smells like burning sulfur."

"Yikes," I said, laughing.

"Exactly." Jacob patted the spot next to him. "But I also kind of wanted to run into you."

Eeeee!

I slid onto the bench and faced Jacob.

"Nervous about the show tomorrow?" he asked.

"So nervous," I said. "I don't want to embarrass my team."

"Sasha, I don't know anything about horses, but I know *you*. You work hard. You're not going to embarrass anybody."

"I hope not." My cheeks flushed.

"You won't." Jacob put his hand on top of mine. "You're freezing. You better go."

I nodded. "Yeah, I've got to get ready for tomorrow."

"Good luck—let me know when you win!" He moved his hand from mine and picked up *Tom Sawyer* again.

When I got back to Winchester, I found Paige in the common room kitchen.

The air smelled like freshly baked bread.

"What're you making?" I asked.

"Homemade cinnamon rolls with icing," Paige said. "In case . . ."

"In case what?" I looked at Paige a little closer. Hairs stuck out of her sloppy ponytail and she had flour on her collar. Her recipe notebook was open and she had six recipes scratched out with a red pen, notes written all over the margins, and a sticky note that said RE-DO ALL RECIPES stuck to the counter.

Paige hesitated. "In case I need a new recipe for the next *Teen Cuisine* tryout."

"No!" I said. "No way. You've got this. I know it. You're *going* to win."

Paige gave me a small smile. "You sound so sure."

 169

"I *am*. I'm going to say 'I told you so' when you win."
Paige's smile broadened. "Deal."

The timer dinged and Paige busied herself with taking the rolls out of the oven and inspecting them.

Now that she was happy, my mind wandered to regionals. Tomorrow was show day. Tomorrow, Charm and I would be chasing blue!

CHASING BLUE

IT WAS FOUR-FIFTEEN ON A BLACK MORNING when I stumbled down the Winchester hallway. Regionals were finally here! I was so excited, I hadn't even hit the snooze button once.

I tiptoed down the eerily quiet hallway. On my way out, I saw something fluttering under the heating vent in the ceiling. As I got closer, I saw that it was a 3-D paper heart suspended from the ceiling with fishing wire.

THE SWEETHEART SOIRÉE IS ALMOST HERE.

NO TIME AND NO PLACE? DON'T BE WORRIED—NEVER FEAR!

FINE, WE'LL TELL, PAY ATTENTION MY DEAR.

IN THE BALLROOM AT EIGHT, JOIN IN THE CHEER!

A new Soirée clue! I couldn't wait to see if Callie had seen one in Orchard.

The cold air made me shiver in my stable coat. It couldn't be warmer than forty degrees. The campus was almost more beautiful in the dark, with its black lanterns lighting the sidewalks and the buildings glowing softly against the dark sky.

As I approached the stable yard, I blinked in the dim lights and saw exactly what I had expected—complete and utter craziness.

"Mr. Conner!" Alison whined. "Sunstruck won't let me wrap his tail!"

"But Mr. Conner!" Julia called from Trix's stall. "I can't get Trix's travel boots on!"

Mr. Conner put down a stack of blankets and headed for Alison's stall. "Be there in a sec," he told Julia.

I slipped out of Charm's stall—he was already blanketed, wrapped and calm—and headed for Trix and Julia.

I knocked on the door and popped my head over. "Can I come in? Maybe I can help."

Julia brushed her hair out of her eyes and waved me in distractedly. "I can't get these shipping boots on the right way." She handed me the black boot with Velcro and buckles all in the wrong direction. I untangled them and bent down by Trix's gleaming black leg.

"She looks great," I said. I petted her left leg before fastening the boot.

Julia knelt down and watched me buckle the straps. "Thanks. She works really hard. I just hope it pays off." I got up and ducked under Trix's neck and then got on my knees for the second boot. I peered under her stomach and looked at Julia. Preshow jitters must have got to her. She never had trouble with boots before. "You guys practiced every second. You'll do great."

"Thanks," she said.

As soon as I left Trix's stall, Mr. Conner motioned to me. "We're ready to load Charm," he said.

I hurried to Charm's stall, clipped a lead rope on him, and led him outside.

"See you in a bit, boy." I hugged his neck and he leaned into me. Mike took the lead rope and Charm stepped into the van.

"Five minutes, everyone!" Mr. Conner's voice rang over the campus. I'd been running around so much all morning, I hadn't even gotten a chance to chat with Callie.

I waved at her as she came over. "Let's ride with Mike

and let the Trio go with Mr. Conner," she suggested.

I nodded. "You read my mind."

We hopped into Mike's truck and waited for him to get inside. This was it—we were going to regionals! I reached in my pocket for my lucky show-day lip gloss. Well, I hoped it would be lucky. I'd bought it online last week. I smoothed the Bonne Bell cookie dough shine over my lips and passed it to Callie. She applied the gloss and handed it back to me.

"Here we go," Mike said, climbing into the cab. A CANTERWOOD CREST hat was pulled low over his freckled forehead. He smiled at us and started the engine.

Callie and I looked at each other as the van crawled forward and we started down the long, winding driveway.

My heartbeat raced. Regionals, here we come!

"We're here!" Callie squealed a little more than an hour later.

Mike eased the truck up a long gravel driveway and pulled into a grassy parking area. Four trailers pulled in behind us—there were already hundreds of horses and riders roaming the grounds.

Callie and I hopped out of the truck and onto the city

of Fairfield's show grounds. The Trio got out and walked over to us.

"Girls, go ahead over to the check-in tent," Mr. Conner directed us. "We'll unload the horses."

I looked around and spotted a white sign with CHECK-IN TENT in red letters.

We set off toward the tent. Vans, trailers, trainers, riders and horses were everywhere. It was orderly chaos. I watched a groom lead a Hanoverian and a Dutch Warm-blood down a trailer ramp. The unloading area was a sea of colored blankets that protected horses from the chill.

I can't believe Charm's competing against horses like these, I thought. But Charm could take them.

We got in line for the check-in tent and I sneaked a look at the Trio. They'd certainly win blue for Best Groomed Riders. Heather and Alison had French braids. Clear polish coated their nails (no color—show rules) and they each had sparkly coats of pink lip gloss. As much as it pained me, I'd have to ask them what kind it was later. We were still in jeans and coats, but after we checked in, we'd change into our show clothes. I knew theirs would be the best from the new Dover catalog.

"Well," said a voice behind me.

I turned. A tall girl with dark chocolate brown hair

smirked at us. She had little braids woven throughout her hair and wore skinny jeans tucked into black paddock boots. Her eyes were focused on Heather.

"Heather," she said. "Wow. I had no idea you were coming *here*."

Heather tilted her chin up a notch. "Well, *Jas*, it shouldn't be such a shock. After two summers at Spencer's Riding School, you must have noticed I was the better rider."

Jas smiled. Pale pink blush sparkled on her fair cheeks.

"Um," Julia said. "What school are you from?"

"It's *Jasmine* and I ride for Wellington," Jasmine replied.

My eyes widened. Wellington was the top boarding school in New York. The school had a reputation for crushing victories in the New York horse show circuit competitions.

"Don't be rude, Heather," Jasmine said. "Introduce me!" Heather sighed. "That's Alison, Callie, Julia, and Sasha."

"Where's the rest of your team?" Alison asked.

Jasmine stuck out a glossy bottom lip. "They were supposed to be here, but they all got food poisoning last night. Insane, right? So, I had to come by myself." She

smiled without smiling. "Oh, well. I'm here to represent Wellington and I'm sure I'll be enough for the scouts."

Callie and I shot each other a glance. A warning sign flashed before my eyes: KEEP JASMINE AWAY FROM FOOD.

"This campus is gorgeous, isn't it?" I asked, changing the subject. "Union doesn't have any grounds like this."

Jasmine froze, staring at me. "No way," she said. "You're from *Union*?"

"Yeah," I said, looking at the other girls.

"Oh, my God." Jasmine laughed. "What's your show record? Like, country fairs and cow tipping?"

"N-no," I said. "I came to state last year and—"

"And what?" Jasmine cut me off. "Lost horribly? God, it's not like Canterwood's in the same class as Wellington or anything, but at least it's not a total dump."

"Whatever!" Alison said, folding her arms and glaring at Jasmine. "Canterwood is *the* best school in Connecticut."

My feet felt rooted to the ground. I wanted to walk away, but I couldn't move. I tried to say something—anything. But I couldn't.

Jasmine shook her head. "Right. I'm sure you'll do great today, Sasha," she said. "I'm sure riding ponies under the circus tents at Union prepared you for—"

"Shut up and get out of her face," Heather growled.

Jasmine's grin slipped. "Excuse me?"

"You heard me." Heather stared into Jasmine's eyes. "Go harass someone else. You're being pathetic."

Um . . . was *Heather Fox* sticking up for me?! Julia and Alison eyed each other; Alison gave a small shrug. Callie looked at me and raised an eyebrow.

"Fine," Jasmine seethed. "But you'll be sorry. I guarantee it." She smiled at us and dropped back behind Alison. She immediately pulled out a BlackBerry and started texting—probably telling her friends there was an actual Union resident on campus.

When we finally got up to the check-in booth, it was only a few minutes before our registration was complete. We picked our numbers up off the table, which we'd have to pin those on the backs of our jackets later.

As the five of us headed back to our trailers, I kept my eye on Callie. I could tell she was more nervous than she'd let on because she was chewing on her thumbnail, her telltale sign.

"What do you have first?" Callie asked.

I looked down at my schedule. "Show jumping," I read. "I'm going to go walk the course."

"Right," Callie said with a nervous smile. "See you later."

"I've got to walk, so I'll come, too." Julia said to me.

Julia and I were the only Canterwood riders in this show jumping class. We had to walk the course and pace our jumps before our rides.

We went to the indoor arena and walked inside. Fluorescent lights supplemented the weak sunlight that had begun to light the building. A handful of riders walked the course. One guy trotted from jump to jump and counted the strides under his breath.

Julia and I walked through the ring's entrance.

"Tough one," I said, getting my first look at the course. It looked more difficult than it had on my diagram. The turns were tighter, the jumps seemed higher and the order of the course seemed confusing.

"Look at the distance between those oxers," Julia said.

"That turn will be tricky," I said.

We walked to the first vertical and I counted strides in my head. I'd have to be on my game to get Charm over this course without knocking a rail. The twelve jumps weren't going to be easy. Julia's face scrunched as she counted strides.

"Is something up with you and Callie?" Julia asked.

"What? No. I don't think so."

"She seems tense," Julia said, shrugging.

"I guess she's just stressed about the show. Maybe it'll help when her mom gets here."

Julia nodded.

"Are your parents coming?" I asked.

Julia looked at me as if deciding whether or not she actually wanted to have a conversation with me.

"My mom is," Julia said finally. "Dad had to work. Yours?"

"Both. I couldn't talk them out of it even if I wanted to."

"At least your parents *want* to come," Julia said. "No one's coming to see Heather ride." She clamped her mouth shut. "Repeat that and die."

"I won't," I promised. "But . . . can I ask you something?"

Julia gave me a look like she couldn't have cared less what I did.

"After the way Mr. Fox gets on her case, he's not even coming. Why?"

"Too busy or something," she said. "But he sent her new Ariat boots to make up for it."

"Oh," I said. Ariat boots were amazing, but I knew Heather would rather have had her family there cheering her on.

We made another lap around the course.

"We should get changed after this," Julia said when we got to the middle of the course.

I nodded. "Four, five, six," I counted under my breath.

Julia's phone rang. "Oooh, hiii!" she squealed.

I whipped my head around to look at her. She didn't talk to Alison or Heather like that. And then I realized . . . Ben.

Julia glared at me.

I walked away, but stayed close enough so I could hear.

"I miss you, too," she said. "I will, thank you. I'm going to win for you!"

I glanced at her, but she ignored me and put her phone in her pocket. Usually, Julia was all business before a show. Maybe Callie should have the you're-getting-distracted-by-boys talk with her for once.

"Was that Ben?" I asked, trying to sound casual.

Julia looked at me. "What do *you* know about Ben?"

"I know he's your boyfriend," I told her. "Was that him?"

She smiled. "Yeah, it was."

"Is he coming to the Sweetheart Soirée?"

"Of course! We're meeting there. I told him I'd kill him if he's late."

I laughed. "You probably scared him into getting there half an hour early!"

Julia and I smiled at each other and we went back to focusing on the course.

Forty minutes later, we were all changed and ready to tack up. I checked my watch. Mom and Dad would be here soon. Mom had called three times last night to tell me she and Dad were leaving Union early to be sure they got good seats in the stands.

Julia and I reached our temporary stabling area and split up. I found Aristocrat's stall before I reached Charm's.

I poked my head over the stall guard. Heather was inside, tightening Aristocrat's girth.

"Heather?"

She narrowed her eyes at me. "God. You're always just . . . there."

I rolled my eyes. "I just wanted to say thanks," I said. "For back there with Jasmine." Heather waited. "For standing up for me?" I prompted.

"I didn't do it for *you*." Heather pulled down the left stirrup iron. "I just didn't want anyone on our team rattled. Jasmine can't beat us!"

"Whatever," I said. "At least we agree on one thing—no way can she beat us. See you later."

I found Charm's stall and tacked him up. My phone buzzed and I pulled it out of my pocket.

Sasha Silver: I hope you get this text. Didn't want to call in case it wasn't allowed. Your mom and I are in the show jumping stands. Love, your dad (Jim Silver)

Like I had a dad with another name! I giggled at the message. It was obviously the first text Dad had ever sent.

"Sasha!" Mr. Conner called as I slid two fingers under Charm's girth and checked it. "You've got twenty minutes to warm him up and get over to the show jumping ring with Julia."

"Thanks, Mr. Conner," I said. "We'll be ready."

Across the grounds, Julia led Trix in circles. Her mom, Mrs. Myer, had just arrived. She stood off to the side and watched her daughter, looking comfortable in khakis, a black trench coat, and a sweater. She shared Julia's tiny build.

Julia halted Trix and wiped her hooves. Mrs. Myer motioned toward the show jumping ring and after a nod from Julia, walked off in that direction. Mr. Robb—Alison's dad—had arrived at the same time as Mrs.

Harper—Callie's mom—had and they'd hurried over to watch Alison and Callie's classes.

It was a bummer I couldn't watch Callie, but Charm and I had to prep. I thought about Julia's question earlier about Callie—maybe it was better that I couldn't watch her after all. I remembered that she'd always been tense before big shows, but she seemed even more competitive than usual lately. Better to just give her her space today.

"You can head over to the show jumping stadium anytime," Mr. Conner told me.

Charm and I started forward. He pricked his ears and rolled his eyes as he stared at the campus. At Union, most of the grounds were small and packed. The area for regionals was *huge*. Dozens of rings, eight or nine buildings, and at least five parking lots were packed with people and horses. The cream-colored barns were stark against the winter sky.

"Julia, I'm heading over," I said. "You coming?" She finished rubbing Trix's legs with a cloth and then passed it to Mike. "Sure."

Julia's compact mare took short, quick steps and snorted as Julia led her forward. Trix was definitely ready to go!

We were headed to the arena when Jasmine walked by.

She led a rangy gray gelding whose nostrils flared at the sights around him. "Ready to lose?" she asked.

"Are *you*?" Julia retorted.

Jasmine's horse swished his tail angrily as he passed Charm and Trix, but Julia and I pulled our horses forward and kept walking. Psych-out tricks were nothing new at these shows.

When we reached the stadium, Julia walked Trix up and down an empty aisle. I bent over to check Charm's bell boots. Our favorite boots were the glitter jelly ones that came in dozens of colors but, at shows, Mr. Conner didn't let us use those. Instead, Charm wore plain, boring black. I knew he'd rather be wearing his favorite baby blue ones.

Mr. Conner strode into the arena and motioned for Julia and me to come over.

"All right. Julia, you're on deck first. Sasha is seventh," he said. Jasmine was riding fourth, so I'd get to watch her ride before I took the course. "Any questions?"

"No, sir," I said. Julia shook her head.

Mr. Conner smiled and put a hand on each of our shoulders. "I'm proud of both of you. Go out there and do your best. You've made Canterwood and me extremely proud."

My eyes misted for a second as I straightened and dusted off my jacket sleeves. Mr. Conner didn't talk that way often, so it meant more when he did.

Julia mounted Trix and rode to the ring's entrance.

Regionals, round one: Here we go!

Julia and Trix waited at the starting line.

I crossed my fingers that Julia would have a good ride for Canterwood. The bell sounded and Trix cantered forward to the first jump. Trix seemed to glide over the course and Julia handled her with ease. Their time was fast—before I knew it, they only had two jumps left.

Julia eased Trix before a tall vertical. Trix's stride shortened too much and she took off a half second late. Her hooves clipped the rail and brought it down behind them—an automatic four faults. Julia didn't get rattled though. She stayed cool as she got Trix over the final jump. She patted Trix's neck and relaxed the reins, slowing her to a trot and heading out of the arena.

"Good ride," I said, grabbing the reins so Julia could dismount.

"Not really," Julia snapped. She hopped to the ground and patted Trix's neck. "Good try, girl. You didn't mess up—it was me."

I looked back at the course. Another rider was headed for the starting line. No matter what Julia said, Canterwood was off to a good start. I hoped I could do as well as she had done.

Two more riders completed the course. Both had four faults—just like Julia.

"Next is Jasmine King riding Phoenix," the announcer said.

A bell sounded and Jasmine entered the ring. She pointed Phoenix at the first jump, a red and white vertical, and the gelding took it easily. They cleared the second, third, and fourth jumps without hesitation. Jasmine urged Phoenix forward and let him lengthen his stride before the flowerbox. Phoenix hesitated a stride before takeoff and Jasmine tapped his flank with her crop. The gelding took off unevenly and his choppy takeoff didn't help his landing. His back hooves nicked the flower box and the plastic rail tumbled to the ground.

Four faults.

Phoenix was rattled, but Jasmine did her best to collect him. His ears flicked wildly back and forth. Jasmine tried to calm him with her hands, but before she could get his attention, they were a stride before the liverpool. Phoenix dug his hooves into the ground and slid to a stop.

Judges penalized heavily for a refusal. Four faults were tacked onto their score. Jasmine circled him and got him over the liverpool on the second try. Phoenix took the rest of the jumps with ease and Jasmine guided him with confidence.

On the final vertical, Jasmine's head snapped up toward the crowd for a second and then she heeled Phoenix into a slow gallop. The course wasn't big enough to gallop!

"What's she doing?" I asked Mr. Conner.

He frowned and shook his head. "Showing off."

I squeezed my eyes shut and listened to the quick thud of hoofbeats. I did *not* want to see an accident on the course.

Phoenix's gait was too fast. The horse got excited and fought for rein, causing Jasmine to lose control for a split second. Phoenix vaulted over the fence at an awkward angle. Jasmine yanked harshly on the reins and tried to get him under control, but she was too late. His hooves thunked against the rail and brought it crashing to the ground. Four more faults for a total of twelve for the ride.

"She got lucky," Mr. Conner fumed. "She could have hurt that horse or herself. The judges will probably speak with her after class."

I nodded. The higher up I moved through the show

circuit, the more reckless riding I'd seen. Jasmine hadn't even been thinking of Phoenix's safety during that ride.

She hurried Phoenix through the exit and dismounted, quickly handing her horse off to a waiting groom. Phoenix, exhausted by his mad dash, hung his head as the groom started to cool him. Mr. Conner would never have let us get away with riding like that *or* not caring for our horse.

Julia and I watched the fifth rider, a thirteen-year-old on a chunky quarter horse mix, take the course and end with four faults. The sixth horse had trouble at the stone wall and threw her rider. Automatic disqualification.

To take the lead, Charm and I couldn't have any faults. There were three riders after us, so we had to get a low score and a good time.

Charm stood at the starting line and I leaned down by his ears. "Whatever happens, it's like Mr. Conner said. I'm so proud of you."

Charm grunted and took a deep breath. I tensed in the saddle and waited for our signal. This was it. I kept my eyes off the crowd. By the rail, Mr. Conner eyed the course and then looked at me. He gave me a thumbs up.

Diiiing!

The bell shrilled and I urged Charm into a canter. *You can do this, boy!* I wanted to tell him, but I focused my gaze

forward and sat quietly in the saddle. We popped over the red-and-white vertical. Okay, one down.

Charm cantered gamely toward the second jump—an oxer with white trellises adorned with fake ivy—and we soared over it. The crowd applauded and Charm's ears swiveled toward the noise. "Pay attention," I whispered, increasing the pressure on his mouth. He cantered over the verticals, flowerbox, and liverpool. We made a tight turn to take a line of oxers and we headed for the final, and highest, vertical.

We swept around the turn and a bit of foam from Charm's mouth splattered his chest. The course designer had been tricky and had put the highest jump at the end, when the horses were tired. Squeezing Charm forward with my legs, I nudged him with my heels and let him quicken his canter to give him more speed to get over the tall red-and-white rails. If we made it over this one, we'd go clean and would have decent chance at placing.

Five strides away, I counted down. *Four, three, two, one, and squeeze!* I thrust my hands forward along Charm's sweaty neck. He launched over the rails and thudded to the ground—landing heavily and almost falling on his knees. If I went over his head, we were done.

Charm! C'mon! I leaned back in the saddle and tried not

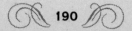

to tug on his head. I felt him fight to keep his footing. Charm gathered himself and surged forward.

Phew!

Charm's near fall left me so rattled, I didn't even know if we'd knocked the final rail or not. Charm cantered out of the ring and he wasn't even at a full stop before I hopped off his back.

Mr. Conner hurried over.

"Are his legs okay?" My hands shook as I spoke.

Mr. Conner unwrapped Charm's boots and checked each leg from hoof to knee. "He's fine. You're lucky the arena dirt was so soft. Cool him out and we'll check them again."

"Oh, Charm," I breathed. I wrapped my arms around Charm. The scoreboard behind him flashed.

1. Sasha Silver/Charm

OMG! "We're number one! Great job, boy!"

"Excellent," Mr. Conner said excitedly. "Well done."

Charm huffed into my ear and I led him off to walk while we waited for the rest of the riders to go. I couldn't even watch. I was too nervous. Julia stood by the rail and called out their scores to me, even though I could hear the announcer. "Eighth rider has eight faults," she said. Then five minutes later, "Ninth rider—disqualified." Either

191

she was trying to help or she was attempting to give me a heart attack each time she oohed and aahed over someone's scores.

I held my breath and waited for the final rider. I buried my face in Charm's mane, unable to look at the arena.

"Last rider . . . ," Julia started. She paced back and forth in the dirt.

"The final rider, Amanda Miller, has a score of eight faults."

"Well, you won," Julia said. She didn't smile. "At least we beat Jasmine."

I turned away from her and looked at Charm.

"Charm!" I said. "We did it!" I hugged him hard. He lifted his head at the applause and let out a throaty nicker.

"You did great, too," I said to Julia. "Third is amazing!"

"Yeah, third." Julia's shrugged. "Wow."

Julia wasn't used to coming in third—especially not to me.

Charm's tail swished proudly as we collected our blue ribbon.

"Nice ride," the judge said, smiling. He patted Charm's shoulder.

The ribbon fluttered on Charm's bridle. I wondered if he'd get mad when I took it off—he could be very possessive about his ribbons. Jasmine tugged a ribbonless Phoenix out of the arena.

The judge pinned the yellow on Trix. Julia smiled at him and shook his hand. Together, we rode out of the ring and up to Mr. Conner. He held up a palm to each of us. We rode by and gave him high-fives.

"Wonderful job, girls," he said. "Callie and Heather both won their dressage classes and Alison picked up fourth in hers."

"All right!" I cheered. I'd forgotten that Heather had decided to show at a higher-level dressage class than Callie this time—it was amazing that they'd both won!

I couldn't wait to see Callie—or Mom and Dad! Canterwood was stealing the show.

"C'mon," Mr. Conner said. "We need to give the horses a break before you two have your last class. And I've got to get to the hunter hack ring."

I touched Charm's ribbon with my finger. We both tried not to prance out of the arena, but I couldn't stop Charm. His tail swished from side to side and, as we reached the door, he let out a triumphant neigh.

20

AN OFFER
THEY CAN'T
REFUSE.

BEFORE LUNCH, I WALKED THE CROSS-COUNTRY
course with Heather and Mr. Conner. Pacing cross-country
was superimportant. I had to know the course to get Charm
safely over the jumps. It had also given us a chance to esti-
mate our time and figure out where we could shave off seconds. Unlike show jumping, nicking a jump didn't equal a
penalty. But refusing, taking a jump out of order, going in
the wrong direction, or falling were all chances for penalties
or elimination. If you rode over the time limit, that also
meant faults.

Afterward, Callie and I grabbed lunch and brought it back
to the stable to eat. I was starving—and I hadn't even had
a chance to talk to Mom and Dad until now.

"Way to go, honey!" Mom said, handing me a pink blanket from her oversize bag to sit on.

"Thanks, Mom," I said, taking the blanket and spreading it in the empty (and clean!) stall. I looked up at her over the stall door and wondered if this was what Charm felt like when he was in his stall. It felt cozy and private and the walls kept us away from the madness going on in the stable.

"I heard you did great too, Callie," Mom said.

Callie beamed. "Thank you!"

I devoured my turkey sub and then started on my chips.

"Where's your mom?" Dad asked Callie, peering into the stall. A hunter green Canterwood Crest sweater peeked out from Dad's leather jacket.

"She's on the phone outside the stable, telling my dad about the show."

Callie had been a little quiet since we'd started eating, but she looked relaxed now.

"We took so many pictures," Dad said, brandishing his camera. "These'll look great in the Silver family newsletter!"

"Da-ad." I shook my head, but Callie laughed and I couldn't help smiling.

"We're going to get lunch with the other parents," Mom

said. "But we'll see you out on the cross-country course."

Dad popped his head farther over the door and took a final picture of us.

"Dad!"

"Going, going," he said.

I turned to Callie, who was finishing her plain hot dog. She hated *all* condiments.

"Can you believe we both won?" I asked.

Callie snorted. "Actually? Yeah. We practiced really hard. When's your next class?"

I checked my watch. "An hour. I've got to tack up and get over there soon. You?"

"Thirty-five minutes. It's hunter hack—with Alison."

I redid my bun and winced when the bobby pins poked into my scalp. "I'm with Heather this time."

"Isn't Jasmine in that class, too?"

My nose wrinkled at the sound of her name. "I think so."

If I lost to Jasmine, Heather would kill me.

I balled up my sandwich bag and frowned. "She's probably ticked that we're doing so well."

"I hope so!" Callie wiggled her eyebrows up and down and we giggled. Finally, she took a deep breath and stood up. "I'm going to head over. Good luck."

"You too." I stretched out on the blanket while I finished my drink. The soda bubbles helped to soothe my stomach.

I decided that this was just what I needed—a moment to myself. I'd been running around since four this morning from grooming, calming Charm and helping Mr. Conner. I just needed to shut my eyes for a second. . . .

"Sasha! Sasha!" Mike stood over me. "Wake up! You start cross-country in twenty-five minutes!"

"What? Oh, my God! I fell asleep!" Charm wasn't even tacked up—now I'd be late and miss my class! I'd blown it!

Who falls asleep in a STALL?!

"Take it easy," Mike said. He offered me a hand and pulled me up. "Charm's ready, but you need to go grab Heather and take your horses to the warm-up ring. Mr. Conner will meet you over there in a few minutes."

"Thanks, Mike!" I left him and found Doug holding Charm at the end of the stable. Doug handed me my protective vest and I buckled it on.

Charm and I hurried to Aristocrat's stall. I looked over the red stall guard and saw Aristocrat was untacked.

"What are you—" I started. Then I saw it. Something was wrong with Aristocrat's coat.

Greasy liquid dripped off Aristocrat's coat and fell to the ground. Clumps of sawdust were rubbed into his coat. He looked like an oil slick!

"Oh, my God," I said. "What happened?"

Heather whipped around and the dripping cloth she clutched splattered oil onto the stall wall. "Jasmine happened!"

"No way," I said.

"I know it was her—this is totally her M.O.," Heather said.

I stuck a tacked up Charm in the empty stall next door and came back to Heather.

"She did this because of me," I said. "You stood up for me and she oiled Aristocrat. I'm so sorry."

Aristocrat had his head down. He flicked an ear dejectedly at the sound of my voice.

"Poor guy," I said. I rubbed his cheek—the only part of him that wasn't oily. He squeezed his eyes shut and let me pet him.

Heather shoved a handful of towels in my direction. "Help me get this off! I can't wash him—it's too cold. If I don't get to cross-country, I'm out. I'm NOT going to lose because of Jasmine King!"

I started sopping up the oil from Aristocrat's coat. If

I'd been like Heather, I would have laughed and headed for cross-country, leaving her to deal with her mess. After what she'd done with Jacob, she deserved it. But I couldn't. She was still my teammate and I couldn't bail on her like that.

For ten minutes, we used dozens of towels and mopped the oil off Aristocrat's darkened coat. Soon, we had a pile of dirty towels at our feet and Aristocrat didn't look so slippery.

"We've got to go," I said, looking at my watch. "Can we tack him up?"

Heather took one last swipe over his barrel and nodded. "We have to try."

She tossed an absorbent saddle pad over his back. Together, we lifted the English saddle and set it down on top of him.

"The girth won't slip, will it?" I asked.

Heather shrugged. Oil speckled our arms and we had sticky sawdust on our sleeves. At least the judges wouldn't be able to see that on the cross-country course.

Heather tightened the girth and reached up to tug on the pommel of the saddle. The saddle didn't slip.

"I think we're okay," Heather said. The color started to return to her face. She slipped the bridle over Aristocrat's head and I grabbed Charm from his stall. We shoved on

our helmets and tightened the straps on our cross-country protective vests.

We led them out of the stable and mounted. The horses moved into a trot and we hurried toward the warm-up arena.

Heather looked over at me. "Thanks," she said.

"Sure," I said, surprised.

When we reached Mr. Conner, he put his hands on his hips and stood between our horses.

"Where were you?" he questioned.

"I'm so sorry. I fell asleep and——" I started

"Well, Aristocrat got dirty——" Heather said at the same time.

He shook his head and put up a hand to stop both of us. "Never mind. Let's go or you'll both be late. Remember what we talked about? Absolutely no rushing. These jumps are solid. I'd rather have a safe round with a slower time than have you be reckless. Got it?"

Heather and I nodded. Mr. Conner was right——risking an injury to win wasn't worth it.

"Head over there and I'll meet you in a few minutes," Mr. Conner said.

Heather and Aristocrat trotted forward, leaving me behind.

"I can't believe we made it," I said. Charm's ears flicked back at my voice.

"Silver, be quiet," Heather said. "I'm trying to concentrate on visualizing the course."

"Sorry."

The cross-country area had been roped off so spectators wouldn't wander into the riders' paths. Judges were stationed around the course, usually out of the rider's eyesight. Half of the battle of cross-country was staying seated. The other half was enduring the grueling jumps and making good time.

Charm and I would go before Heather and Aristocrat. I rode Charm in serpentines while we waited for Mr. Conner. While Charm moved, I tried to visualize the course. What did I do about the bank jump? Did we canter fast or slow up to it? I looked for Mr. Conner, but he wasn't here yet. What if he didn't make it before I went? Something could have come up at the stable. I started to ask Heather, but she was deep in concentration, tracing the course in the air.

Charm was sensitive to my moods. If I got upset, it would make him jittery. Over the hill, I saw Mr. Conner's head. I flopped onto Charm's neck with relief.

I trotted Charm over to Mr. Conner.

"You okay?" he asked.

"The bank jump," I squeaked. "I'm really nervous about it. Slow or fast canter?"

"Sasha, you know Charm," Mr. Conner said. He blinked against the strengthening sunlight that peeked from behind a cloud. "Trust him. Don't start second-guessing yourself."

"So, a slow canter? Or fast?" I grinned when he laughed.

"Try a slow canter and if you feel short on time, fast will be okay."

"Number 56, you're on deck," called the announcer. That was us!

"Okay," Mr. Conner said. "You're on. Good luck, take your time."

I mounted Charm and nodded to Mr. Conner. "Thank you."

Charm trotted calmly into the starting box. The crowd stirred behind the ropes, but I pushed them out of my head and listened to Charm breathe. I put a bit of pressure on the reins and leaned forward slightly. My knees tightened on the saddle. "You can do this, Charm," I whispered. "Let's go get 'em."

Booong!

The deep-toned bell sounded. I pulled the reins to

the right and dug my right heel into Charm's side. With moves worthy of a barrel horse, he whirled around and cantered forward. We always had to start backward or Charm would bolt forward like a racehorse. We went through the yellow ropes that held back the crowd and headed for the first jump—a stone wall. Charm cantered strongly toward the three-foot high wall and leaped over the gray stones. The red flag was on our right, so I knew we'd at least taken the first jump in the right direction.

Charm snorted, tugging at the reins, and picked up his speed as we cantered over several yards of grass before approaching a brush fence. He hopped the fence and we entered the woods.

"Easy," I said. I slowed his pace a fraction so I could peek at my watch. Right on time. We swept down a winding trail littered with acorns and flashed by a judge. Sunlight cast strange shadows in the woods—I'd have to make sure none of the shadows spooked Charm.

We thundered over a log jump and soared over an old park bench with peeling red paint. Charm cantered on flat ground out of the woods. His breathing quickened and his coat started to darken with sweat. I checked his stride and slowed him as we cantered up and down several rolling hills designed to test his endurance.

We hit flat ground again and cleared a picnic table. Charm was doing amazing! He was sweating and blowing a bit, but he didn't hesitate before any jump.

"We're almost there, big guy!"

The bank was next. Charm dug deep and found an extra burst of speed. I leaned back in the saddle as we cantered down the embankment and the creek rushed at us. The fast-moving water foamed as it rushed around rocks and surged around a bend. *Three, two, and over!* I squeezed with my knees and Charm lifted over the water and scrambled up the other side, which was torn up and muddy from horses who had stepped in the water.

We turned and cantered in a half circle. I lifted slightly out of the saddle to take pressure off Charm's back and to give him a break. The final three jumps popped into view. "Just a little more, boy," I said, glancing down at my watch. We'd lost a couple of seconds in the woods and needed to get over these fences and gallop to the finish line. "Ready to finish this?"

Charm stretched his neck and his legs struck the ground faster. "Let's go!" We cantered over a metal gate, a water jump and were strides away from the trakehner. The trakehner required the horse to trust the rider. This jump had two rustic rails in front of a wooden ditch that looked like a coffin. A ditch was one jump that usually caused the most run-outs or refusals, so Charm had to believe I wasn't going to let him fall into the scary box.

Charm's rhythmic strides pounded the grass. I shoved my heels down into the stirrups to help my balance. The reins rubbed against the sweat breaking out Charm's neck despite the cold. The rubber grips on my gloves kept my hands steady on the reins. We had seconds left on the clock, but I wasn't going to push him. He'd done too much for me to force him to rush to the last fence when he was exhausted.

Charm's body didn't even tense before the trakehner. He tucked his knees and arched over the rails and the ditch. "Good, boy!" I leaned forward and kneaded my hands along his neck. Charm's mane whipped in my face as he flattened into a ground-eating gallop and powered over the finish line.

Charm was giving his all for me. I thought of the sound his heart had made when I'd listened to it with the stethoscope. My horse had the biggest heart here.

Our time flashed on the board. We were two seconds off the maximum time, so that meant we'd racked up .8 of a penalty. Not bad for our first go at regional-level cross-country.

Heather trotted Aristocrat over to us. I hopped off Charm and loosened his saddle. "Nice job," she said. She gave me a half-smile. "That's a great score."

"Thanks," I said, leading Charm forward and away from the course. "You up soon?"

"Three riders to go and then me," Heather said. "You should come back and watch."

I turned back and nodded. "Maybe I will."

Charm nickered tiredly as we walked away from the noise. White foam had formed around his saddle pad and the corners of his mouth were flecked with froth. His chest was darkened with sweat. He kept his head low.

"You were amazing, boy. You did everything I asked."

"Sasha!" Dad called as he and Mom caught up with us. "We were in the crowd by the picnic table. That was amazing, sweetie!"

"I was watching with my eyes half closed," Mom added. "That was a big jump!"

"Charm did all of the work," I said. "He deserves a long rest." Mom rubbed Charm's neck and took his reins so I could lean into Dad. My legs were wobbly. I couldn't even imagine how tired Charm felt. I knew our time hadn't been fast enough to earn a ribbon, so I'd leave Charm at the stable when I went back to watch Heather ride.

"Excellent ride," Mr. Conner said, stepping beside me. He had a light blanket folded over his arm. He shook it out and put it over Charm's back. "Get him untacked, cooled, and check his legs for heat. I'm going to Alison's class, but call me if you need to. Make sure you take Charm to the vet box."

Half an hour later, Charm was cool, dry, and taking a few slow sips of water under the watchful eyes of Mike.

Julia and Alison walked Trix and Sunstruck around the yard to cool them down after their class.

"Hey!" I called as Callie walked over. She and Jack were done for the day, but she had to untack him and assist Mr. Conner.

"Alison got first in her class and Julia got *second*," Callie whispered.

"Really? Wow!" I said.

"I know! You going to watch Heather?"

"I'm on my way right now," I said.

"Call me if anything happens."

"I will."

I left Callie and headed toward cross-country. I weaved through the crowd of people with umbrellas, blankets and lawn chairs.

When the bell sounded, Aristocrat shot out of the

starting box. Heather guided him easily over the stone wall and they disappeared into the woods. I walked through the grass and found a clear spot near the course's end. I plopped onto the cold grass and drew my knees to my chin, snuggling into my coat.

While I waited for Heather and Aristocrat to finish the course, I texted Jacob.

First place!! :o) I typed.

A second later, my phone chimed.

Told you! Congrats!!!

I wanted to break into a nerd dance. *Three* exclamation points.

It didn't take Heather and Aristocrat long to emerge from the woods. When they raced toward the finish line, I knew their time had been waaaay faster than Charm's and mine.

Heather guided Aristocrat over to me after his vet check and we waited for the judges to announce the winners.

"Good ride," I said.

Aristocrat's sides heaved as Heather walked him in circles.

"Thanks." Heather took off her helmet and snapped it onto one of Aristocrat's stirrup irons.

"How sad that you're still here," a voice snipped.

Heather and I turned. Jasmine had one hand on her hip and the other on Phoenix's reins. I'd missed her ride when I'd been cooling Charm.

"You really think you placed, Heather?" Jasmine asked. "At least Sasha was smart enough not to even bother bringing her nag for the ribbon ceremony."

I'd had it. She could insult me, but no one dissed Charm.

"Charm is NOT a nag!" I yelled. "Don't ever call him that again. I'm not like you. I wouldn't push him or risk an injury to win."

"Please," Jasmine said. "He's just a horse."

"Well, I bet my horse beat yours," Heather interjected in a sweet voice. "But you totally helped me."

"What?" Jasmine narrowed her eyes.

Heather stepped closer. "The oil you put on Aristocrat helped us glide over the course. Right to the blue ribbon."

Jasmine's mouth opened and closed.

"Thanks for that!" Heather chirped with a giant smile.

Jasmine pulled Phoenix away to wait.

"And now, the ribbons are to be awarded for cross-country," the announcer said.

"Third place goes to Abigail Hille on Orbit, for Priestly

Day School," the judge announced. A short girl on a leggy mare accepted her yellow ribbon.

"Second place goes to . . ." Heather and Jasmine glared at each other. "Jasmine King on Phoenix, for Wellington Prep."

A smattering of applause broke out. Jasmine tugged poor Phoenix forward and snatched the red ribbon from the judge's hand. She crumpled it into her hand and disappeared off the course. I blew a silent breath of relief.

I stuck out my hand by my knee and gave Heather a low high-five.

"Our first-place rider is Heather Fox on Aristocrat, for Canterwood Crest Academy," the judge said.

"Congratulations!" I said.

Heather smiled and patted Aristocrat's neck. They headed up to the judges. The judge held out a hand to Heather. She shook his hand and returned the smile. Heather took the ribbon and held it in front of Aristocrat. The gelding lowered his head and nosed it.

A grin crept over my face. Heather *did* deserve to win cross-country. Sure, after the show, everything would go back to normal between Heather and me. But at least we'd pulled it together for today. For Canterwood.

The rest of the results went up on a wooden announce-

ment board. Charm and I had snagged fifth place. Not bad!

"Excellent, excellent job, girls," Mr. Conner said. He smiled at us, but his attention was on Aristocrat. "Let's get him cooled. When you're finished, I want you to come out by the van, okay?"

Heather and I nodded. Mr. Conner walked off and we followed behind him. I was just glad Jasmine was gone. She made even Heather look nice. I never wanted to see her again!

"Sorry your mom and dad couldn't come," I said to Heather as she led Aristocrat back to the stable.

"Whatever," she snapped. "I didn't want them here anyway."

"Oh," I said, wishing I'd kept my mouth shut.

"But I'm glad I won," Heather said, her voice softer now. She straightened and looked at me. "I proved to my dad that I don't need him in my face to win. I win because I'm good."

The last sentence could have sounded cocky or like Heather was bragging. But she wasn't. She *was* good. The moments when she acted like a human and not an Ice Queen were few, but it gave me hope. Maybe we had a shot at being civil to each other more often.

"Yeah," I said softly. "We were both good today."

With that, we walked in silence the rest of the way to the stable.

The Canterwood riders were officially dirty, cold, and ready to go home.

"Bye, Mom and Dad," I said, hugging them one last time.

"Great job today, honey," Mom added.

"We love you," Dad said.

I waved as they headed for the car.

Callie's mom, as pretty as Callie with her same dark features and long eyelashes, hugged Callie again.

Heather stood off to the side while Mr. Robb kissed Alison's forehead and Mrs. Myer practically crushed Julia with her enthusiastic hug.

The horses were bandaged, blanketed, and ready for the trip back to Canterwood. I knew Charm couldn't wait to get back in his old stall and sleep. We were both taking tomorrow off and I'd hand-walk him on Monday instead of riding him. He'd worked so hard and I wanted him to get enough rest.

The five of us gathered around Mr. Conner.

"You've all done well today." Mr. Conner smiled. "Several other instructors noticed your rides and commented to me that I've got a strong, capable team."

We looked at each other.

"I've kept this quiet until now, but during midwinter break, I'll be overseeing an intensive and exclusive clinic at Canterwood. Various instructors from other top schools in New England will be teaching different areas in the clinic. Competitive riders from other schools will be staying at Canterwood for the clinic. Only a few select riders will be offered slots."

Callie and I eyed each other.

"I want to extend seats to the five of you and your horses. If your parents agree to allow you to spend midwinter break at Canterwood, I'd love for you to attend."

"What?" Alison said. "No way!" Julia clasped her hands.

"I take it that you're interested, then." Mr. Conner smiled.

"I'm in!" I said. No way Mom and Dad would say no. Charm and I would learn a million things from the clinic!

"Me too!" Heather added.

Julia and Callie nodded.

"Good," Mr. Conner said. "Talk to your parents and get their permission. It won't be an easy week, but you'll

learn a lot. Let's load these tired horses so we can get them back home."

I went to Charm's stall and clipped a lead line to his halter. "You did great today, boy," I said. I stroked his blaze and rubbed his neck. "Change of plans for midwinter break. I won't be going home and you won't be eating all day and hanging out with Jack." Charm gave me an evil eye. "But I'll be staying with you and we'll be riding in Mr. Conner's clinic."

I leaned into Charm and he bumped me with his muzzle. I kissed the end of his blaze and hugged him.

My phone vibrated in my pocket. I took it out and peered at the lit-up screen. Paige!

"How'd you do?" she asked. Her voice was squeaky.

"First in show jumping and fifth in cross-country," I said proudly.

"Sash! That's great!"

"I'm really excited! Plus, guess what?"

"What?"

"Mr. Conner invited the Trio, Callie, and me to a clinic at Canterwood. Charm and I are staying on campus for midwinter break!"

"Wow!" Paige squealed. "That's awesome. But it figures."

"What?"

"I was going to stay on campus for break, but I can't now."

"Why?"

"Because . . . I got a call today from The Food Network for Kids!"

"No!" I screamed. Charm cocked his head toward the phone. I held it close to his ear so he could hear, too.

"Yes! I got it! I'm the new host of *Teen Cuisine*!"

"PAIGE! OMIGOD!!"

"I have to go to New York City over break and tape the shows," Paige said. "That's why I can't stay on campus."

"That's the best reason EVER," I said.

Paige laughed. "We'll have to celebrate double victories tonight."

"Get the movies ready," I said. "And the chocolate. And the chips."

After we hung up, I took Charm's blue ribbon from my coat and pinned it on his halter. He'd want to wear it on the van ride home just in case Aristocrat gave him a hard time.

21

NOT JACOB

OVER THE PAST TWO DAYS, I'D DEVELOPED AN unhealthy new obsession. I couldn't stop staring at the blue ribbon over Charm's stall. I'd put it up on Sunday morning and could barely tear myself away.

"Are we going to trail ride or are you going to make out with your ribbon?" Callie teased.

"Well, blue *is* my color," I said, laughing. "I'm ready."

Mr. Conner had canceled all riding practice for the week after the show. I was glad—I needed a break from drills and it had been forever since Callie and I had hit the trails. More than anything, I was glad to ride with Callie when we weren't training.

We led Jack and Charm down the aisle and out in front of the stable. There was a light dusting of snow on the ground. Callie and I had coated the insides of our horses' hooves with petroleum jelly to keep the snow from balling up inside their hooves—we didn't want either horse to wrench an ankle. We mounted and I looked behind me. I'd draped a rug over Charm's hindquarters and it was snug under the saddle.

The sky above us was the darkest gray I'd seen all winter. The sun, barely visible through thick clouds, didn't provide any warmth for the four of us. We kept the horses to a walk as their hooves crunched the frozen grass. I shivered in my coat and pulled the collar up higher.

"Paige swears it's going to snow," I said, my breath visible.

"Nah," Callie said. She shook her head as she guided Jack next to Charm. "It's just gloomy. Did you talk to your parents about the clinic?"

"Not yet. I wanted to wait until after I got my bio homework back. If I'd gotten a bad grade, they would have wanted me home to study over break." It had killed me not to blurt out the clinic invitation to Mom and Dad, but I'd known better. Now I had all the ammunition I needed to convince them to say yes.

"What'd you get?"

"A-minus."

"All right!" Callie leaned over and high-fived me. "Call them now!"

"Okay!" I pulled my phone out of my pocket and dialed. "Mom?"

"Sasha?" she said. "What's going on? Is everything okay?"

"Everything's fine," I said. "I just have a favor to ask."

"Uh-oh," she said, her tone light.

"No—it's good. It's *really* good. Mr. Conner is teaching a midwinter break riding clinic and he asked if Charm and I could participate. I'd have to stay on campus over midwinter break."

I held my breath.

"Hmm," Mom said. "How are your grades?"

"As and Bs. Mr. Ramirez won't screen my documentary until after break, but I'll definitely get an A."

Next to me, Callie crossed her fingers.

"It must be important if Mr. Conner wants you to stay."

"It is!" I enthused.

Mom laughed. "Let me talk to your dad. I say yes and I'm sure he will, too."

"Thanks, Mom!"

We said good-bye and hung up.

"It sounded like a yes to me," Callie said.

"Mom said okay and Dad will definitely agree with her." I patted Charm's neck.

With sighs of relief, we settled back into our saddles and enjoyed the peace of the trail ride.

Charm and Black Jack walked quietly over the frozen ground. The trees were damp—a thin layer of ice coated even the skinniest branches.

"What do you think the clinic will be like?" I asked.

Callie pursed her lips. "I don't know. The only one I attended was for the New England Saddle Club. We had different instructors for dressage and jumping. They each had their own style and you had to learn how to take criticism from a bunch of different people."

"Sounds hard," I said. "But good for training."

"Plus, we'll be working with new riders," Callie said. "That'll be different . . . for you."

"Yeah," I said. "I guess it'll be weird."

I tried to shake off the strange tone in Callie's voice. I'd thought she'd just been anxious for regionals and that's why she'd been acting so strangely. But now regionals were over, and things still felt off. Almost like . . . I tried to shut my brain down before it finished the thought, but I wasn't fast enough:

Almost like she thinks she's a better rider than me.

I let Charm move a half-stride ahead of Jack.

"You know we'll have to try extra hard to stand out from the other students," Callie said. She pushed a snow-covered branch out of her way.

"We'll do great. We just have to stick together like we always do," I said. But I wasn't sure if she'd heard me—she was still looking straight ahead, like she was thinking about something else.

A light snow started to fall and the sky began to darken from a light grayish blue to a darker steel. I fought off a shiver and tried not to worry about Callie. She was probably just nervous about the clinic. I mean, she was still my BFF—nothing could change that. Could it?

By the time Callie and I turned back to the stables, the sky was even darker and a biting wind was blowing over campus. Even for February, it felt too cold.

Inside the stable, I untacked Charm and took Black Jack's tack from Callie. I lugged both saddles and bridles to the tack room. Callie watched our horses until I got back.

"How about a massage?" I asked Charm. "You deserve one after last week."

Charm nodded and tugged on the crossties.

"I've got to go," Callie called from outside of Jack's stall. "See you tomorrow."

"Okay," I called. "See you . . ." But Callie was already gone.

The stable was quiet for a Tuesday afternoon. Most of the horses were tucked away in their stalls with light blankets. Mr. Conner had all of the doors shut, including the big door at the main entrance, and heat blew through the stable.

I pushed my fingertips into Charm's back and he sighed. Horse massages were the hottest new trend according to *Equestrian Journal*.

Thinking about riding with Callie at the clinic made me nervous. What if I looked like a beginner next to all of the new riders?

Boots thudded down the aisle and I looked up and saw Eric, sporting jeans and a charcoal gray jacket.

"Hey," he said, reaching out to touch Charm's muzzle. "Congrats on the win. I heard you were amazing."

"Thanks," I raised my voice to a stage whisper. "But you better congratulate Charm, too. He gets offended easily."

"Oh, right," Eric said. He turned away from me and faced Charm. "You did great, sir."

Charm snorted and accepted a cheek scratch.

"So, I wanted to tell you thanks for everything," Eric said.

I looked at him. "Everything?"

Eric shrugged. "You know, I'm the new guy. It's hard to start school in the middle of the year. You made it easy for me to be comfortable here."

I nodded. "I know what that's like. Not everyone was nice to me when I got here. But I'm glad we're friends."

"Right," Eric said. "Friends." He gave me a half-smile.

"Yeah." I smiled.

Eric picked up the body brush from my tack box and flicked it over Charm's shoulder.

Okay, *that* was weird. Had Callie been right? Did Eric think we could be *more* than friends? Immediately, I dismissed the idea. Man, I was really reading way too much into things lately. Eric didn't *like*-like me, he just . . . liked me.

"So . . . are you going to the Sweetheart Soirée?" I asked. The Soirée was on Thursday. I'd thought this close to Valentine's Day, everyone would be chatting nonstop about it and more flyers would appear. But that hadn't happened. I hadn't heard anyone talk about it for a couple of days, and no one had seen any new signs or flyers anywhere.

"Probably," Eric said. "None of the Blackwell guys know anything about it, so I kind of want to go just to see what happens!"

I nodded. "Me too. My friends don't really know anything about it either. And the one girl who probably knows everything is going out of her way not to tell me."

Eric laughed. It was easy to talk to him. I looked at him and for a second, I thought about Jacob. I wished Jacob could stand next to Charm and talk to me about the party or the details about the show the way Eric could. I knew that wasn't fair because he wasn't a rider, but still. All I really wanted was to *talk*.

Eric placed the brush back in my tack box. "Well, then . . . I'll see you at the party?"

"See you then," I said.

I grabbed Charm's green blanket off the counter and fastened the Velcro ties over his chest and girth. I unclipped him from the crossties and we walked into his stall.

I checked his water bucket, refilled his hay net and took off his halter. "Night, boy," I said. I stroked his mane and gave him a hug. "See you tomorrow."

Charm ignored me and headed straight for his hay. He began munching before I was even out of the stall. If only all boys were as easy to figure out as Charm.

22
2 GUYS + 1 GIRL
= TROUBLE

"I'M SOOO SICK OF TUNA SURPRISE," CALLIE said. "*Every* Wednesday!"

"Agreed," I said. "What's the surprise, anyway? The fact there's no tuna in it?"

We laughed and headed for our lunch table.

"Hey," Paige said as we plunked down our trays.

Callie jammed a couple of tater tots into her mouth. "So . . . hungry," she said through a mouthful.

"Can I sit with you guys?"

We all looked up at Eric. Callie froze—her cheeks puffed up with tater tots. She swallowed hard, her face red, and squirmed in her seat.

"Sure!" I said. "Have a seat."

Eric put his tray on the table and sat down across from me.

Callie straightened her necklaces and ran a hand through her hair.

"So, you're a victim of tuna surprise, too," I said.

Eric grimaced at his tray. "Usually, I make my own sandwiches, but I didn't have time today."

Paige put down her water glass. "You make your own sandwiches? What kind?"

"Different ones—like pepper beef or chicken provolone."

"You're gonna regret saying that," I said in a teasing tone. "Paige is *the* master chef. Now she'll be hitting you up for recipes."

Paige leaned closer to him. "How do you make your pepper beef?"

Eric laughed with me, but turned to Paige to give her his recipe.

Callie picked up her tray and stood. I looked over and saw that she'd barely touched any of her food.

"Where are you going?" I asked.

"To class," she said. "I'm not up for watching two guys fight over you," she added in an angry whisper.

"What are you talking about?"

I followed Callie's glare behind me and saw Heather and Jacob enter the caf. Heather's arms were loaded with books. She whispered something to Jacob and he took the books from her. I felt my face grow hot as their hands touched. Then, Jacob saw me and smiled. He gave Heather back her books and started to walk over to me. He paused momentarily when he saw Eric sitting across from me.

Jacob slammed his books onto the table. "Hey, Sash." He took a seat next to me. "Don't you usually sit at a different table?" Jacob asked Eric.

Eric took a long swig of Coke. "Sometimes. But I like this table. I might sit here more often."

I looked at Paige with *help me* eyes.

"Uh, so, Jacob," Paige started. "What class do you have next?"

"English."

"I've got math," Eric told me. "Too bad we're not in the same class, but at least we can hang out at the stable."

Jacob set his jaw.

I coughed as I found myself choking on—surprise—a bit of tuna.

"Too bad Sasha's going to have less time at the stable

after break—we'll be screening movies for film class," Jacob told Eric. "Together."

"Um, I've got to get to class," I said.

"Me too!" Paige said.

We got up and both Eric and Jacob stood at the same time.

"Bye, guys," I told them. "See you later."

Before either one of them could follow us, Paige and I darted across the cafeteria, tossed our trash, and hurried down the hallway.

"That was *insane*," Paige said.

"I know! And I think Callie's mad at me because she sort of likes Eric. But I never *told* him to like me! I like Jacob."

"Do you think that has anything to do with how weird she's been acting?" Paige suggested.

And even though I knew it was totally crazy, even though the thought had never even crossed my mind before now, and Jacob was still the only guy I had any interest in going out with—I knew Paige was right.

Callie was mad because she thought I liked Eric.

23

GET THE PARTY
STARTED

THE SWEETHEART SOIRÉE WAS JUST UNDER
two hours away.

Paige and I were in full-blown panic mode. It was after
six and we'd been prepping since school had let out at
three thirty. We'd ordered dresses online a couple of weeks
ago and had spent hours sifting through them before we'd
found *the ones*. Sweetheart-spectacular dresses.

"Ready?" I called from the bathroom.

"Ready!" Paige said back from the bedroom.

We'd made a pact not to see each other in the dresses
until we'd both had them on. We'd seen them online, but
it was different in person. We'd adhered to the dress code
Paige had seen on a new flyer—pink or red for the girls
and black and white for the guys.

"One, two . . . three!" I said and pulled open the door.

"Sasha! Wow!" Paige gasped.

I twirled in my bright pink dress. It had skinny silvery spaghetti straps. The fabric swirled around my hips and skimmed the tops of my knees.

My mouth flopped open. "*You* look amazing!" I told Paige.

And she did. The strapless baby-pink dress had a gorgeous, pearly white sash that made Paige's waist look enviably tiny. She looked totally Oscar-ready.

"Thanks," Paige said. "I love this dress. I'm keeping it forever!"

We giggled. Paige pulled me over to her desk—the top wasn't even visible. She'd turned the workspace into a beauty counter. Foundation, lip gloss, brushes, cotton balls, and mascara tubes were everywhere. Paige's bed was covered with plastic containers full of accessories.

"Makeup first and then jewelry," Paige said. "I'll do yours and you can do mine."

Paige put on a pair of glasses with purple plastic frames.

"Since when did you start wearing glasses?" I asked.

"They're fake," Paige said. "They make me feel like a makeup artist."

"Oooh. How very artsy of you."

"For this session, you may call me Jade," Paige said.

I laughed. "Deal."

"Tinted moisturizer first," she said. She pumped a dime-sized dollop into my hands and I smoothed it on my face.

Paige peered at me through her glasses and grabbed soft gray eyeliner and a tube of mascara from her Clinique zip-up bag. "Your skin is perfect so you don't need foundation or powder. We'll line your eyes, put on a bit of mascara, a dab of blush and lip gloss, and you'll be good."

"Okay, Jade," I said.

"Close your eyes."

I obeyed and let her work her make-up magic.

When she was done, I peered at my face in the mirror. I loved what I saw. Smoky gray eyeliner set off my green eyes and a dusting of soft pink blush made my skin look like it was glowing. Paige had coated my lips with a shiny clear gloss so that my eyes were the focus.

"Wow," I breathed. "Amazing. Okay, your turn."

I got out of the desk chair and waved a hand for Paige to sit.

I looked into the makeup bag for shimmery eye shadow that would match Paige's dress.

"Wait," she said. "What's your name, makeup girl?"

I tossed my hair and thought for a minute. "Kiki," I said finally.

Paige laughed and settled into the chair while I went to work.

After I'd finished Paige's makeup, it was accessory time.

"Borrow whatever you want," Paige said, sifting through the boxes of watches, rings, earrings and necklaces.

"How *did* you get all of this stuff? Are you an eBay addict, Paige Parker?"

Paige laughed. "Parties and friends of my parents. It's expected to give the daughter a gift whenever you come over to visit."

"Wow. My parents need new friends."

I pulled out a pair of delicate silver earrings and held them up to the light. Wisps of thin silver dangled down in swirls. "How about these for you?"

Paige held them up to her ears and looked in the mirror. "Perfect."

She handed me a silver bracelet with a heart charm. "Wear that and you're set," she said.

I clasped the bracelet around my wrist and Paige put a silver ring on her index finger.

"Hair, shoes, and then we're ready!" I said. My stomach swirled like Paige's earrings. Jacob would be there.

We'd hang out and finally have time to laugh and talk without the pressure of grades and the show. Maybe we'd even dance again—or hold hands.

All I wanted from tonight was to have fun.

Paige and I stood outside the Canterwood ballroom. Every window of the two-story building was lit up. The scent of cinnamon and vanilla wafted through the air. A boy our age walked in ahead of us wearing a suit. I couldn't help staring. I'd never seen any Canterwood student wearing a suit before.

"You sure we're ready for this?" I asked Paige.

I looked down at my shoes—strappy black shoes with kitten heels—and ran a hand over my straightened hair.

"It's just a party," Paige said. But she kept playing with her earrings like she always did when she was nervous.

"So, we'll go in and . . ."

". . . party," Paige finished.

"Right." I laughed. "Party. Okay."

Tonight, the high school kids had their own party in a separate, secret location, so I wouldn't feel too weird interacting with the older kids.

Paige and I had walked from Winchester and the starry sky had been clear and the night air was cold. Behind us, gray clouds built in the distance. We had a fifty-fifty shot at rain tonight.

Paige pulled open the doors and we stepped into the toasty lobby.

"Coats?" A man in a black uniform (he had a *hat*) extended a white-gloved hand.

"Omigod," I whispered to Paige. "They went all-out for this!"

"I know," Paige whispered back as we handed off our coats. "And we're not even inside yet."

Paige smoothed her wavy hair with her hand and we walked across the carpeted entrance to the double doors. Music and laughter trailed out of the room.

"Let's go," Paige said. With that, she put a hand on the door and pulled it open.

"Oh . . ." she started.

". . . my God," I finished.

We stopped, frozen in the doorway. Every inch of the ballroom had been transformed. White curtains flowed from the windows and the black-and-white marble floor glinted. There was crystal-like glitter on the floor that sparkled like a million diamonds. Ivory tablecloths covered round and square tables. This looked like a Hollywood party!

Every guy was dressed in black, white or both. Most

were in suits with white or black ties. Girls were in pink or red dresses.

"Look up," Paige whispered to me.

My eyes went to the ceiling. Hundreds—no, *thousands*—of pink, black, and white balloons were against the ceiling, floating around the crystal chandelier. On the far wall, a banner read SWEETHEART SOIRÉE in curly lettering.

"There's Callie!" Paige said.

Callie looked, well, NOT like Callie. Her long hair was piled on top of her head in a sophisticated up-do. She had on a bright red minidress that poofed at the bottom like a ballerina tutu. Her shoes were red ballet flats and a silver horseshoe-shaped necklace draped around her slender neck glittered under the lights. She'd swiped on clear lip gloss too, and a coat of mascara. I barely recognized her!

Callie looked away, almost like she was thinking about pretending she didn't see us, before she ambled through the crowd.

"Hi," Paige said.

"Hey." Callie gave us a brief smile before shifting from one foot to the other.

"Wow, we all look great!" Paige added.

Callie and I just nodded. This was too weird—was she really still mad about the Eric thing?

"So, we're supposed to check in. Then, I think we can do whatever we want until the dance," Callie said.

I didn't even know what to say to my best friend!

Paige and I followed Callie over to a table where one of the eighth grade teachers sat. He was in a coat with tails and had on a black top hat.

"Hi, girls," he said. He smiled at us and picked up something off a big table next to him. "Take these," he said. He handed Paige and me each a small red box.

I opened mine. Inside, nestled on a white swatch of satin, was half of a silver heart with jagged edges—almost like a key.

"When we make the announcement," the teacher said. "Find the other half of your 'broken heart' so that you have your one dance together. Have fun!"

I noticed Callie already clutched one of the broken hearts in her left hand.

"These are so cool!" I said.

"Wow, they must have cost a fortune," Paige said.

I scanned the room for Jacob.

"I haven't seen him yet," Callie said. "But he'll be here."

"Have you seen Eric?" I asked Callie.

"Not yet."

I hoped Eric would be Callie's match—maybe she

would see that I didn't like him and it would melt some of the awkwardness between us.

"Let's get drinks," Paige suggested.

We walked across the shimmery floor to the punch table. I noticed the Trio in a comfy nook of the room.

They all wore shades of red, but Heather's crimson dress was the darkest. The one-shoulder dress looked more dramatic than Julia and Alison's cherry halter-top dresses. A thin gold choker glittered around Heather's neck. Julia and Alison wore matching oversize red and black rings on their index fingers.

Julia and Ben had squeezed together into an oversize chair. He looked cute in a black tux and white tie. He held her hand and nodded at everything she said. Alison and Heather had their hands together and passed a folded piece of paper between them.

Callie's eyes followed my gaze. "Don't they look cozy."

"Yeah," I said. "A little too cozy."

At the drink table, different crystal bowls filled with pink and red liquid glimmered up at me. Instead of plastic cups, like the ones I'd used at the riding team's winter party, there were long-stemmed glasses and white cloth napkins.

Following Paige's lead, I took the ice tongs and dropped a few heart-shaped ice cubes into my glass. I

poured pink lemonade over the ice and watched the hearts bob to the top.

"You're going to be the party star," I said to Paige.

"Oh, I forgot about that!" Callie said. "You get a special announcement from Ms. Drake about *Teen Cuisine*, right?"

Paige blushed and nodded. "At the end of the party."

I pushed away my annoyance—at least with Paige, Callie was acting normal. So I guessed it was just me. It felt like Callie and Paige were BFFs tonight!

"I'll scream and cheer for you," I said. "Maybe 'Paige Parker—the new TV diva' or something like that."

Paige's eyes widened. "You better not."

I gave her a wide-eyed *Who me?* look and took a sip of lemonade. Suddenly, someone touched my elbow. I turned . . . and there he was.

"Wow," Jacob said. "You look great."

"Thanks," I said. "So do you." And he did. He'd totally pulled off the dressy-cool Hollywood look: unbuttoned black suit jacket, long-sleeve white shirt, and a pair of black pants. He looked amazing.

"Hey," Jacob said to Paige and Callie.

They smiled at him and then pretended the drink bowls were fascinating.

"Have you ever been to a party like this?" I asked.

Jacob shook his head. "Never."

"I bet even my parents haven't been to a party like this," I said.

This felt so good. Just Jacob and me. Chatting, like last semester.

"Hi, guys."

I sighed when I recognized the voice.

"Hi, Heather," I said as I turned to face her.

"You guys ready to ditch this party until the dance?" Heather asked.

"Depends," Jacob said. "What did you have in mind?"

What?! Why would he even *think* about doing something Heather suggested?

Heather flashed a smile. "Julia, Alison, and a few other riders are in the back room. It was supposed to be locked, but one of the teachers must have left it open. Come hang out with us."

I looked at Paige. This reeked of trouble.

"Look—" I started to say.

"Okay," Jacob said at the same time.

Callie nodded and stood by Heather. "Let's go."

Paige and I hadn't moved. But what choice did I have now? I didn't want Jacob to leave without me and he obviously wanted to go.

"Fine," I said.

"But how do we sneak out of here?" Paige asked, eyeing the chaperones.

"Follow me," Heather said. She glanced around the room and pointed to the group of chaperones who had gathered by the snack table with their backs to us. Heather motioned us forward and we followed her to a black door that was almost hidden by a flowing white curtain from one of the big windows. Heather twisted the knob and pulled the door open just wide enough for us to squeeze through.

"Hurry up!" Heather hissed.

Jacob watched over our shoulders as Heather, Callie, Paige, and I slipped inside. Finally, he darted through the door and pulled it shut.

Alison, Julia, Ben, and Eric were sitting on a red couch pushed against a wall. Troy and Andy sat on the edge of a big coffee table.

"Hi, Sash," Eric said.

Callie frowned and twisted the bracelet on her arm as Eric walked over to me. His dark hair was pushed back off his forehead. He looked polished and—I'll admit it—handsome in blank pants and a white dress shirt.

"When did you get here?" I asked nervously.

"Ten minutes ago," Eric said. "Heather pulled me in here—she told me she was grabbing you guys."

"C'mon, Sasha," Jacob said. He stepped up beside me. "I'll get you a chair."

"Thanks." I smiled at Eric and then watched as Jacob strode over to the side of the room and pulled two folding chairs from along the wall. Troy and Eric grabbed chairs for Callie and Paige and we arranged them in a lopsided circle by the couch.

Paige sat beside me and Jacob hurried to sit in the chair on my other side. Eric sat beside Heather on the couch. He barely looked at Callie. If only he knew how much she liked him! Boys. So clueless.

"Let's play Truth or Lie," Heather said. She scooted to the couch's edge.

"Yeah!" Alison said. She bounced on the couch cushion. "I love that game!"

"How do we play?" Paige asked.

"It's easy," Heather said. She reached into her black purse and pulled out a stack of white note cards. "We're each going to write a truth and a lie on a piece of paper anonymously. Try to hide your identity so it's not an easy guess. Like Paige wouldn't write 'I've got red hair' as a truth and then make up a lie."

"That ruins it," Julia interjected.

Heather gave her a how-dare-you-interrupt-me glare. "Then we mix up the note cards in a bowl and draw. You read your note card aloud and then you try to figure out whose card it is and what's the truth and what's the lie. If the guesser gets the truth, lie, and person right, you have to confirm it."

"Okay," I said. "Let's play." This could be dangerous.

Heather handed everyone a note card and swiped an empty pretzel bowl off the coffee table. We all took a minute to write our truth and lie. Troy's tongue stuck out of the corner of his mouth as he crossed out some writing and scribbled another line.

One by one, we all handed our cards to Heather. She tossed them into the bowl and swirled them around.

"You pick first," Heather said, thrusting the bowl at Alison.

Alison reached inside and felt around before pulling out a card. She smiled.

"Okay, it says, 'Once, I let my annoying cousin drink a glass of water AFTER I'd watched my cat drink from the glass.'"

We all laughed—that was a good one.

"Then it says," Alison continued. "'Last week, I watched

the *I Wanna be a Pop Star* 2 marathon on TBS.'"

Alison shifted to look at all of us. "Julia," she said. Julia's poker face was *awful*! She blushed and twirled a lock of short hair around her index finger. Ben elbowed her and she hid her face in his shoulder.

"Your truth is," Alison started, "you let your cousin drink cat spit and you lied about watching *Pop Star*."

Julia nodded. "You got it."

"Ewww!" Callie said, laughing. "How could you let her drink that?"

"Easy," Julia said. "She said my Ralph Lauren skirt was ugly, so she deserved to swap spit with an animal who licks herself."

"Oh, man," Troy said. He looked at Jacob, Eric, Ben, and Andy. "We've got to watch out for these girls!"

"Ben's next," Julia said. She held out the bowl to him and he picked a card.

"It's says, 'I've got a secret crush' and 'Once, I ate a cricket on a dare,'" Ben read.

He looked around and his eyes wavered between Andy and Eric. "Eric," he finally said. "You . . . have a crush and you didn't eat a cricket."

Eric's smile gave him away. "Right."

Jacob's head whipped around to look at Eric. He

opened his mouth and then his phone rang. He peered at the screen.

"It's my dad," he said. "If I don't answer, he'll get mad." He flipped open the phone. "Dad? Hold on. I can't hear you."

He got up and walked to the door. "Still can't hear you. Wait a sec."

The door shut behind him and the game resumed.

"My turn next," Heather said. The rest of us sat back and watched her pick a card.

She read the card and a gleam filled her eyes, then vanished. She sat up straighter and held the card between her red-painted nails.

"It says . . . 'I've never kissed a guy before' and 'My parents sent me to boarding school because I embarrassed them.'"

Phew—not my card. I'd written *I sleep in Tinker Bell pajamas* (lie!) and *I want to audition for a movie someday* (truth)—harmless stuff that Heather couldn't use against me later. She probably expected me to reveal a deep, dark secret. No way!

Everyone stared at Heather while she read the card to herself and looked around at us. Maybe the card was Alison's. But why would she say such personal things about her family situation? Or her lack of kissing experience?

Heather tapped the card against her palm. "I think this card belongs to . . . Sasha."

I almost said, "No," but I shrugged. If I denied it, she'd insist more that it was mine.

"I think the truth is that you've never kissed a boy and the *other* truth is you didn't understand how to play the game. So, you wrote two truths."

On either side of Heather, Julia and Alison smirked. Troy and Andy looked at their laps.

"Excuse me?" I sputtered.

"You. Wrote. Two. Truths," Heather said. The shimmery eye shadow on her top lids made her blue eyes look even lighter. "The only kiss you've ever gotten is from the Silver family mutt and your parents were embarrassed of your lame shows at fairs and carnivals. They sent you here. Away from them."

My stomach clenched. "That's *not* my card."

"You have to be honest," Heather chided. "You're ruining the game. Is this yours?" She pointed to Alison.

Alison shook her head. "No."

"Jules?" Heather asked.

"Nope," Julia said.

"Callie?" Heather asked.

Callie looked down at her lap. "No," she whispered.

"Well, it can't be anyone else's, so it's Sasha's."

Tears pricked my eyes.

"Heather." Eric leaned forward, his voice low. I'd never heard him speak in that tone before. "Leave her alone."

Heather put the card on her lap. "Stop trying to protect her, Eric. We all know Sasha hasn't kissed Jacob yet."

My fists clenched, fingernails digging into my palms. I hated her.

Heather turned to me and smiled. "That's okay, Sasha. Don't worry about it. I can vouch for Jacob . . . he's a really, *really* good kisser."

"Cut it out!" Eric shouted. "Now!"

My vision blurred. I'd known all semester something had been going on between Heather and Jacob. Paige and Callie had tried to convince me nothing was wrong and that I was being paranoid. They were wrong! I'd known it in my gut for weeks. But that didn't prepare me for hearing it. Heather and Jacob. Kissing. All semester.

Callie's eyes lowered and she slumped into her chair.

"Yeah, c'mon," Andy added. "It's a game—it's supposed to be fun."

"I've had enough *fun*," I sputtered. "I'm out of here."

"Sasha!" Eric and Paige said at the same time.

But I ran out the door, forgetting to look for teachers, and stepped back into the crowd.

Heather won't stop for one night! I screamed in my head. *But calm down. She could be lying about kissing him.* No, she HAD to be lying. If I could find Jacob and ask him now, he'd tell me the truth.

I folded my arms and looked for him, but he must have still been on the phone somewhere.

"May I have your attention, please!" Mr. Davidson stepped into the center of the party and tapped his microphone.

No! I wanted to shout. I needed to talk to Jacob now, not dance! I headed for the exit. It was better to leave than suffer through a dance. I didn't want to be here anymore.

"Sasha?" Ms. Peterson called. I stopped with one hand on the door.

"Yes?"

"You can't leave until after the dance, remember? No one can leave yet, otherwise not everyone will have a partner."

"Oh. Sorry."

I pulled my hand from the door and with a sigh, turned to face Mr. Davidson. I watched as Callie, Paige, and the rest of the Truth or Lie players slipped out of the room and blended into the crowd.

"It's now time for the Broken Heart Dance," Mr. Davidson said. "Take your broken heart and find the guy or girl who fits. Once everyone has found a partner, you'll dance for one song and then you're free to party as you like. Go mend your broken heart!"

I swallowed a scream of frustration and tried to match my heart with a couple of seventh-grade guys from math class, but they didn't fit. The sooner we all danced, the faster I could get out of here!

Eric had already found his match—a petite eighth grader with a heart-shaped diamond pin on her pink dress. He looked at me and mouthed, "You okay?"

I nodded and kept looking.

"Are we a match, my dear?" a guy who looked like a eighth grader asked. He had a black fedora perched jauntily on his head.

"Let's see," I said. At least *he* was having fun tonight.

We held out our hearts, but the edges didn't match.

"Too bad," he said, tipping his hat to me.

"Sorry." I slipped back into the crowd, trying to forget for just one second that Heather had just humiliated me in front of all of my friends *and* claimed she'd kissed Jacob.

"She's got to be lying," I whispered to myself. *I'll ask Jacob the second the dance is over.* But I still couldn't find him in the crowd.

More people started finding their matches. The guys who were left had grouped together under the Sweetheart Soirée banner.

"Match?" I asked a guy with blond hair. I think his name was Reese—he was in my history class.

He held up his heart and we pushed them together. *Click!*

"Finally!" I said and he let me hold the heart.

"Reese, right?" I asked.

"Yes, Mender of My Broken Heart," he said with a grin.

"I'm Sasha. We're in the same history class."

"It does appear that you and I are both grasshoppers of the Wise Educator."

Huh?

"What?" I asked.

"You know, Mr. Spellman."

"Um," I said. "Right. Okay."

I looked over and saw Callie chatting with an eighth grade guy. Across the room, Paige had found her dancing partner—one of the quarterbacks on the JV football team. Poor Paige. Jocks so weren't her type. Alison and Julia were with two guys I vaguely recognized.

I didn't know if I could do this. The last thing I wanted to do was dance right now.

I turned to Reese. "Sorry," I said. "But I have to—"

"You can't duck out before the dance, Tradition Bucker," Reese said.

Where did he get this stuff?

"But—" I started to protest again. Reese ignored me and put my hands on his shoulders.

The music started to play. I tried to remind myself how I'd feel if Reese ducked out on me. I couldn't be rude. This *was* tradition, and I couldn't embarrass him by leaving. I took a shaky breath and forced the stiffness out of my body. In two minutes, the dance would be over and Jacob would come find me. We'd find a quiet space to talk and I'd finally ask him about Heather. Whatever his answer—I had to know for sure.

"You okay?" Reese asked.

"Fine," I said. I was the worst partner. "Sorry." We moved back and forth on the floor and I tried to follow his steps to the classical music for this dance. Reese winced. I looked down and my left foot was on top of his dress shoe.

"Ugh. I'm so sorry!" I said.

He smiled. "It's okay."

My eyes caught a flash of a deep red dress and long blond hair. Heather tossed her head back in laughter. Who was her partner? I peered around a tall couple blocking my view and saw *him*. Jacob. Dancing with Heather.

That was it.

"I've got to go," I said.

Reese let me go and I tore off toward Heather and Jacob. I slammed into another girl and didn't even apologize as I weaved through the dancers. A waft of lilac body spray almost choked me. Jacob and Heather stopped swaying to the music when they got a glimpse of my face.

"I can't believe you!" I screamed.

"What's wrong?" Jacob asked. He dropped Heather's hand and stepped away from her.

"You're dancing with HER!"

"Sasha, I had to. It's a random draw and we—"

"Just stop!" I yelled.

Jacob reached out to grab my arm, but I wrenched out of his grasp.

Heather stepped back into the crowd and she left Jacob and me in an empty circle on the floor.

"You've been messing with me all semester!" I cried.

"One minute, you really like me and we have fun together. Then you can't wait to get away from me and you act like you never want to see me again."

Jacob took a step back. Hurt flashed across his face, but I didn't care.

"When did I ever act like that?" Jacob asked. No one in the room spoke and the music swelled.

"When we were filming at the stable! You wouldn't get close to me all day and you rushed out as soon as you could."

"Sash—" Jacob's face looked pale.

Over to the side, I saw Callie and Paige. Callie had her lips pressed together. Then I saw Heather. She stood at the edge of the crowd with a smirk on her face. This was exactly what she wanted. I pulled my eyes away from her and looked back at Jacob.

"Sasha, it's not what you think," Jacob said.

"It's not? You're always with Heather and YOU KISSED HER! I never want to talk to you again. You can dance with her the rest of the night. Go ahead—I know you wanted to anyway."

I locked eyes with Heather once more. She blew me a kiss.

"But I didn't—" Jacob started.

I couldn't do this anymore. I turned away from him and walked out the door.

I stumbled down the steps and got three feet out the door when the icy air hit me. My coat was still inside, but no way was I going back.

"Sasha!"

I stopped.

"Sasha," Paige said again. She grabbed my arms. "Calm down. It's gonna be okay."

"No, it's not!" I wailed. "Heather ruined everything!"

Paige rubbed my back. For the first time, I noticed Callie standing wordlessly beside her. "He had to dance with her. He didn't pick her—you know that," Paige soothed.

"He kissed her!" I said, "You heard what she said."

Callie touched Paige's arm and a look passed between them. Paige gave me a sympathetic look before turning to go back inside, leaving Callie and me alone together.

"Heather was lying," Callie said finally.

"What?"

"Jacob told me just now—he doesn't even like her. She made it up."

"No, but he . . . they were . . . she said . . ."

"Heather's always going to be a liar," Callie said. "You shouldn't have listened to her!"

I wrapped my freezing arms across my chest. I started to shiver. Callie was right. I should have trusted Jacob, the sweetest guy I'd ever met, but instead I'd let Heather ruin everything. For weeks, I'd been so consumed in making up stories about what Heather and Jacob were doing together that I'd stopped seeing what was actually happening.

"But they were together all of the time," I said. Tears of humiliation rolled down my cheeks.

"Jacob told me he was tutoring her in math," Callie said. "Heather was so embarrassed about being tutored that she asked Jacob not to say anything. He's a good-enough guy that he didn't tell anyone—even the girl he likes."

"But that day at the stable," I choked out. "He couldn't wait to get away from me! He acted all weird and—"

I flashed back to that day. Jacob staying away from Luna, being nervous about the palomino in the crossties and not petting Charm.

"He's scared of horses," I whispered. "Jacob's afraid of horses."

Callie was quiet for a minute. "Which means he filmed horses for *you* even if he was scared of them."

The door opened and Callie and I turned to look. Heather stood in the doorway. Light streaming out behind her; she looked like an angel. She stood at the top of the steps and looked down on Callie and me.

"Thanks, Sasha," she said.

I glared.

"You made it *so* easy. I didn't have to do a thing to break up you and Jacob. You did this to yourself. I mean, sure, Julia helped when she sent you that pic of Jacob and me in the library."

My stomach twisted.

"Oooh, and Alison made sure I picked the right card for Truth or Lie."

There was nothing I could say. She loved this. I had been horrible to Jacob for no reason. I was the stupidest, most insecure girl on campus.

Heather continued. "Now Jacob thinks you're a crazy, possessive freak. He'll never speak to you again. But don't worry. I'll be there for him."

My brain was too muddled to snap back. I'd acted like someone I didn't even know. I'd just given Heather everything she needed to get Jacob to like her.

Heather turned and went back inside. The door slammed behind her.

Callie and I stood in silence, our breath clouding the air.

"Go back inside," I said. "Paige's announcement."

"Okay, but," Callie folded her arms. "Maybe you should wait for someone to walk you back."

"I'll walk her."

Eric stood beside me—I hadn't even seen him coming. He had a coat in his hand. He slipped it over my shoulders and nodded at Callie. "Go ahead, I'll go with her," he said.

For a minute, Callie just looked at me—her eyes seething. The phrase *If looks could kill* popped into my head. And then she was hurrying back up the steps, the door slamming shut behind her.

Eric and I were left alone in the rain.

"Sorry, I don't have an umbrella," he said.

I just nodded. Raindrops ran down my dress and splashed onto my shoes.

"Ready?" he asked.

I knew I should go back to Callie—to tell her she had it all wrong about Eric. But tonight had been awful enough—and I was suddenly completely exhausted. All I wanted was to go back to my room.

I went to put my hands in my coat pockets, but they weren't where they used to be. I looked at Eric and saw he was just in his rain-soaked shirt.

"This is your coat," I said.

"I know where you live," Eric said. He hunched his back against the cold. "I'll get it back."

I sighed.

"Okay," I whispered. "Let's go."

Eric put a steady arm over my shoulders and we started down the wet sidewalk.

After everything I'd said, I'd never get Jacob back. We were finished. Over. I leaned against Eric, fresh tears beginning to fall.

Behind us, the door banged open. I looked behind me, expecting to see Heather.

But it was him. Jacob stared at me and our eyes locked. He gripped the black railing with one hand, and in the other was my coat. He was furious. I'd never seen him look like this. Rain dripped off the overhang that shielded Jacob from getting wet. Jacob shook his head at the sight of me and Eric and stormed back inside.

Eric's arm tightened around me. "Forget it for tonight," Eric told me. "You've been through enough."

But Jacob had come. Maybe he'd been about to forgive me, but after he'd seen me with Eric, he'd changed his mind. Maybe I'd never be able to convince him now how much I wanted to be with him—but maybe I could.

I didn't know. I brushed wet hair from my eyes and tears collected on my eyelashes.

I slipped out of Eric's grip and took a step forward, but then stopped. I stood frozen between Eric and the building where Jacob had gone back inside. I could turn around and go to Winchester with Eric. I'd save myself the humiliation of trying to apologize to Jacob when he'd never forgive me. Or I could try and hope that even if he never talked to me again, Jacob would listen to my apology.

The drizzle turned to a downpour. It sent shivers down my back. I clenched my jaw together to keep my teeth from chattering.

I turned to Eric. His kind brown eyes blinked at me through the rain. He didn't leave me to go inside and get warm—he was waiting for me. He'd probably sneak inside Winchester and stay with me until Paige got back.

Eric. Jacob. Comfort or apology.

This was my mess and I had to make it right. I had to choose.

Don't miss the next book from

CANTERWOOD CREST

BEHIND THE BIT

May 2009

I NEVER THOUGHT I'D BE *THIS* GIRL. THE GIRL caught between two guys. The girl who stood outside on a rainy Valentine's Day evening and had no idea what to do. Jacob, my first almost-boyfriend, had just slammed the ballroom door in my face. Eric, my friend and *not at all* boyfriend, took even breaths beside me. But that was Eric. Calm and comforting—the same as he'd been all night throughout this horrible mess.

My roommate, Paige, and I had been sooo excited when we'd stepped into the school's ballroom earlier tonight for the annual seventh- and eighth-grade Sweetheart Soirée. Now everything was ruined.

Raindrops bounced off my shoulders and pinged against the sidewalk. The temperature had dropped, and the rain was beginning to change to sleet. I couldn't look away from the door. He *had* to come back.

"Sasha?" Eric asked.

"Jacob's not coming back," I whispered. "I messed up everything!"

"Don't say that. Come on, let's get you inside. I'll walk you back to Winchester."

I finally tore my eyes away from the door and looked at Eric. Concern clouded his dark brown eyes and I realized, just then, how I must have looked. My once-pretty pink dress, now half-covered by Eric's coat, was drenched with rain. My hair, which had been shiny, blow-dried straight, and perfect, was now dripping and frizzed at the ends. I didn't even want to imagine how my face looked—probably puffy, red, and streaked with makeup.

Part of me wanted to stand here until Jacob realized that he needed to hear my apology. But the other part—the rational part—*knew* Jacob wouldn't walk through that door again after the way I'd just accused him.

"Okay," I said, nodding numbly. "Let's go."

Eric put an arm around my shoulders as we walked down the slippery sidewalk. I wiped the cold moisture from my face and tried to hold back tears. But it had been a long night. Eric glanced at me.

"When we get back to your dorm, I'm going to ask your dorm monitor if I can stay. Just until Paige gets back."

I wanted to thank him, and to apologize for ruining his night too, but I couldn't say anything. My brain felt fuzzy and overwhelmed.

Eric steered me toward Winchester, cutting through the slick grass.

Up ahead, two figures passed by under the streetlamp. The sleet blurred their faces, but as we got closer I saw that it was a couple holding hands. Crazy as it was, I still half expected it to be Heather and Jacob.

"Isn't that—," Eric started.

My breath stopped in my throat and I looked at Eric, wide-eyed.

It was Heather, holding hands with Ben. Julia's Ben. Julia as in Heather's best friend. Fifteen minutes ago, Heather had been tormenting me about Jacob. She'd had me convinced that *they* liked each other and that they'd even kissed. She'd obviously moved on already—to breaking up Julia and Ben. But that was what Heather Fox did, wasn't it? I should have known better by now.

I almost laughed out loud, but I didn't even have the energy for that. Fighting with my friends had exhausted me. In that moment, I couldn't stand to look at Heather for one more second. Eric's arm tightened around me. I raised my head as we passed Heather and Ben and forced myself not to look at them. Eric did the same.

We walked the final distance to Winchester. Eric opened the door and we stepped inside. I let the warmth of the dorm wash over me, shaking the rainwater off Eric's jacket as I walked. Livvie, the Winchester Hall dorm monitor, poked her head out of her office.

"Sasha! What are you doing bringing a boy in here?" she asked, walking toward us and folding her arms across her chest. "You know the rules—" Her mouth closed when she got a better look at my face. "What happened? Are you all right?"

"I'm fine," I lied. "Can we talk about it later?"

Livvie nodded. "But you're soaked! You should get into dry clothes before you catch cold."

Eric cleared his throat. "Um, I'm Eric," he said. "I'm a friend of Sasha's. Is it okay if I wait with her in the common room until her roommate gets back?"

Livvie looked at me and then at Eric. "Okay, but just until Paige returns. And you're to sit on separate couches. I'll be checking."

I was too tired to be embarrassed, or even to laugh. But Eric seemed to think it was funny.

"Okay," Eric laughed. "Thanks."

Livvie put her hand on my elbow. "Come find me if you need to talk, okay?"

"'Kay," I whispered. "Thanks, Livvie."

Livvie pointed Eric in the direction of the common room, and I headed for my dorm room to change. Once inside, I left the lights off and sat on the edge of my bed. I waited for a fresh wave of tears, but none came. Just numbness. I remembered that Eric was waiting for me. I was so glad—I didn't want to be alone.

Ten minutes later, I'd pulled my damp hair into a sloppy ponytail, shed Eric's jacket, and hung my rain-soaked clothes over the back of my desk chair to dry. I tugged on a soft, gray, velour hoodie and matching pants and scrounged up a pair of fuzzy pink socks for extra warmth.

The hallway was empty and quiet as I walked back to the common room. I realized that everyone on my floor was still at the soirée.

When I returned, Eric was standing at the counter, swirling spoons inside two steaming blue mugs.

"Hey," he said, his tone soft. "I made us some hot chocolate."

"Good idea," I said, sitting down on the couch. "I'm still trying to get warmed up."

I tried my best to conjure up a smile for Eric as he set a mug down on the table in front of me.

"I'll sit *way* at the end of this one," Eric said, choosing the one that sat perpendicular to the couch I was on. "I'm afraid an alarm will go off if we sit on the same couch."

"It might." I almost laughed. I took a sip of my cocoa and Eric did the same.

For a few minutes, neither of us spoke. We stared at the fireplace across from the couch I was sitting on and watched as a log crackled and turned to ash. The flames cast dancing shadows on the eggshell-colored walls of the room. I drew my feet onto the beige couch and nestled against the arm, finally beginning to absorb the fire's warmth.

"How could I have been so stupid?" I said finally, burying my face in my hands.

"Hey, you're not stupid," Eric said. "Anyone would have believed Heather. I haven't known her very long, but she seems to be pretty good at causing trouble."

"She is, but I still should have known better. Jacob would never kiss her. He'd never hurt me that way. I should have trusted *him*, but no. I *had* to listen to Heather! And now he's never going to talk to me again. Jacob hates me and *Callie's* mad at me because—" I looked at Eric and caught myself. "Because," I improvised, "of something that isn't even true. And Paige isn't here yet!"

Oops. I'd just spilled my guts to poor Eric, who was probably ready to bolt for the door by now. Like he'd wanted to hear any of that!

"Sorry," I said. "That was TMI."

Eric smiled, shaking his head. "You're upset. You're allowed to rant, you know."

"Eric, what should I do?" I asked. "Go find Jacob tomorrow and apologize? What if he won't listen?"

"All you can do is try. If he doesn't let you explain, then it's his problem. He should at least give you a chance."

I took a deep breath and let it out, slowly.

"Okay, maybe you're right. I'll try."

"Good." Eric got up from the couch and went back to the kitchen. He opened the cabinet doors and pulled out a bag.

"What's that?" I asked.

"Forgot the marshmallows," he said.

He offered me the bag. I immediately had a flashback of my last time at the Sweet Shoppe—our on-campus café/bakery—with Jacob. He knew how much I loved marshmallows, and he'd spooned his into my mug when I'd finished mine.

A new wave of tears fell from my eyes. Eric, with a glance at the door for Livvie, stepped across the room and sat beside me.

"Hey," he said gently, "did I miss something? Do you hate marshmallows that much?" His jet-black hair fell over one eye as he gazed at me with genuine concern.

"No," I said. "They just . . . bring back some serious Jacob memories."

"Oh. Sorry."

"You didn't know." I sniffled and tried not to start what Oprah called "the ugly cry." The one with mascara tracks, red eyes, and a Rudolph-bright nose.

"Let me take those." Eric plucked the bag from my hand. "I'll find another snack, okay?"

I took more deep breaths and blew my nose while Eric looked through the cabinets and tried to find something that wouldn't remind me of Jacob.

"So, I've got a problem with Luna," Eric said. He found a bag of baked chips and poured them into a bowl.

"You do?" I sat up straighter on the couch. "What's wrong?" Eric had listened to me enough. The least I could do was try to help with Luna.

He put the bowl on the coffee table and sat on the other couch.

"She wants to canter back to the stable after every lesson. I almost can't hold her back from running right into her stall."

"Uh-oh. She's getting barn sour."

"Barn sour?"

I nodded and plucked a chip from the bowl. "If you let her hurry back to the stable after a lesson, she'll always rush. You have to *make* her walk back. If she gets headstrong, circle her until she calms down."

Eric smiled.

"Don't let her rush through a lesson just to get back to her cozy stall. The more eager she is to go back, the farther away you need to lead her. You have to be in charge."

"Good idea. I'll try it." He picked up a chip and munched. "Where did you learn that?"

"When I was ten, my parents got me this giant guidebook to horses. I read it every—" I stopped and looked at Eric. "You're trying to distract me with horse talk."

"Is it working?"

"Yes," I said, laughing. "It totally is."

"Good. What else was in that book?" He leaned back on the couch as if preparing to be there a while.

"Well . . ."